IT'S *NOT*

SUMMER

WITHOUT

YOU

The Summer I Turned Pretty
VOLUME TWO

IT'S NOT SUMMER WITHOUT YOU

JENNY HAN

SIMON & SCHUSTER BFYR

New York London Toronto Sydney New Delhi

SIMON & SCHUSTER BFYR
An imprint of Simon & Schuster Children's Publishing Division
1230 Avenue of the Americas, New York, New York 10020
SIMON & SCHUSTER BFYR and related marks are trademarks of Simon & Schuster, Inc.
For information about special discounts for bulk purchases, please
contact Simon & Schuster Special Sales at 1-866-506-1949 or
business@simonandschuster.com.
The Simon & Schuster Speakers Bureau can bring authors to your live
event. For more information or to book an event, contact the Simon
& Schuster Speakers Bureau at 1-866-248-3049 or visit our website at
www.simonspeakers.com.
Also available in a SIMON & SCHUSTER BFYR hardcover edition
Interior design by Lucy Ruth Cummins
The text for this book is set in Bembo.
Manufactured in the United States of America
This SIMON & SCHUSTER BFYR movie tie-in paperback edition November 2022
10 9 8 7 6 5 4 3 2 1
The Library of Congress has cataloged the hardcover edition as follows:
Han, Jenny.
It's not summer without you : a summer novel / Jenny Han.
p. cm.
ISBN 978-1-4169-9555-5 (hc)
[1. Coming of age—Fiction. 2. Interpersonal relations—Fiction.
3. Beaches—Fiction. 4. Summer—Fiction. 5. Vacation homes—Fiction.
6. Friendship—Fiction.] I. Title. II. Title: It is not summer without you.
PZ7.H18944It 2010
[Fic]—dc22
2009042180
ISBN 978-1-4169-9556-2 (pbk)
ISBN 978-1-4424-1385-6 (eBook)
ISBN 978-1-6659-3799-3 (movie tie-in pbk)

J + S forever

Acknowledgments

My heartfelt gratitude to Emily van Beek, Holly McGhee, and Elena Mechlin at Pippin Properties, and to Emily Meehan and Julia Maguire at S&S. Thanks also to my first readers—Caroline, Lisa, Emmy, Julie, and Siobhan. I'm so fortunate to know you all.

chapter *one*
JULY 2

It was a hot summer day in Cousins. I was lying by the pool with a magazine on my face. My mother was playing solitaire on the front porch, Susannah was inside puttering around the kitchen. She'd probably come out soon with a glass of sun tea and a book I should read. Something romantic.

Conrad and Jeremiah and Steven had been surfing all morning. There'd been a storm the night before. Conrad and Jeremiah came back to the house first. I heard them before I saw them. They walked up the steps, cracking up over how Steven had lost his shorts after a particularly ferocious wave. Conrad strode over to me, lifted the sweaty magazine from my face, and grinned. He said, "You have words on your cheeks."

I squinted up at him. "What do they say?"

He squatted next to me and said, "I can't tell. Let me see." And then he peered at my face in his serious Conrad way. He leaned in, and he kissed me, and his lips were cold and salty from the ocean.

Then Jeremiah said, "You guys need to get a room," but I knew he was joking. He winked at me as he came from behind, lifted Conrad up, and launched him into the pool.

Jeremiah jumped in too, and he yelled, "Come on, Belly!"

So of course I jumped too. The water felt fine. Better than fine. Just like always, Cousins was the only place I wanted to be.

"Hello? Did you hear anything I just said?"

I opened my eyes. Taylor was snapping her fingers in my face. "Sorry," I said. "What were you saying?"

I wasn't in Cousins. Conrad and I weren't together, and Susannah was dead. Nothing would ever be the same again. It had been—*How many days had it been? How many days exactly?*—two months since Susannah had died and I still couldn't believe it. I couldn't let myself believe it. When a person you love dies, it doesn't feel real. It's like it's happening to someone else. It's someone else's life. I've never been good with the abstract. What does it mean when someone is really and truly gone?

Sometimes I closed my eyes and in my head, I said over and over again, *It isn't true, it isn't true, this isn't real.* This wasn't my life. But it was my life; it was my life now. After.

I was in Marcy Yoo's backyard. The boys were messing around in the pool and us girls were lying on beach towels, all lined up in a row. I was friends with Marcy, but the rest, Katie and Evelyn and those girls, they were more Taylor's friends.

It was eighty-seven degrees already, and it was just after noon. It was going to be a hot one. I was on my stomach, and I could feel sweat pooling in the small of my back. I was starting to feel sun-sick. It was only the second day of July, and already, I was counting the days until summer was over.

"I *said*, what are you going to wear to Justin's party?" Taylor repeated. She'd lined our towels up close, so it was like we were on one big towel.

"I don't know," I said, turning my head so we were face-to-face.

She had tiny sweat beads on her nose. Taylor always sweated first on her nose. She said, "I'm going to wear that new sundress I bought with my mom at the outlet mall."

I closed my eyes again. I was wearing sunglasses, so she couldn't tell if my eyes were open or not anyway. "Which one?"

"You know, the one with the little polka dots that ties around the neck. I showed it to you, like, two days ago." Taylor let out an impatient little sigh.

"Oh, yeah," I said, but I still didn't remember and I knew Taylor could tell.

I started to say something else, something nice about the dress, but suddenly I felt ice-cold aluminum sticking to the back of my neck. I shrieked and there was Cory Wheeler, crouched down next to me with a dripping Coke can in his hand, laughing his head off.

I sat up and glared at him, wiping off my neck. I was so sick of today. I just wanted to go home. "What the *crap*, Cory!"

He was still laughing, which made me madder.

I said, "God, you're so immature."

"But you looked really hot," he protested. "I was trying to cool you off."

I didn't answer him, I just kept my hand on the back of my neck. My jaw felt really tight, and I could feel all the other girls staring at me. And then Cory's smile sort of slipped away and he said, "Sorry. You want this Coke?"

I shook my head, and he shrugged and retreated back over to the pool. I looked over and saw Katie and Evelyn making *what's-her-problem* faces, and I felt embarrassed. Being mean to Cory was like being mean to a German shepherd puppy. There was just no sense in it. Too late, I tried to catch Cory's eye, but he didn't look back at me.

In a low voice Taylor said, "It was just a joke, Belly."

I lay back down on my towel, this time faceup. I took a deep breath and let it out, slowly. The music from Marcy's iPod deck was giving me a headache. It was too loud. And I actually *was* thirsty. I should have taken that Coke from Cory.

Taylor leaned over and pushed up my sunglasses so she could see my eyes. She peered at me. "Are you mad?"

"No. It's just too hot out here." I wiped sweat off my forehead with the back of my arm.

"Don't be mad. Cory can't help being an idiot around you. He likes you."

"Cory doesn't like me," I said, looking away from her. But he sort of did like me, and I knew it. I just wished he didn't.

"Whatever, he's totally into you. I still think you should give him a chance. It'll take your mind off of you-know-who."

I turned my head away from her and she said, "How about I French braid your hair for the party tonight? I can do the front section and pin it to the side like I did last time."

"Okay."

"What are you going to wear?"

"I'm not sure."

"Well, you have to look cute because everybody's gonna be there," Taylor said. "I'll come over early and we can get ready together."

Justin Ettelbrick had thrown a big blowout birthday party every July first since the eighth grade. By July, I was already at Cousins Beach, and home and school and school friends were a million miles away. I'd never once minded missing out, not even when Taylor told me about the cotton candy machine his parents had rented one year, or the fancy fireworks they shot off over the lake at midnight.

It was the first summer I would be at home for Justin's party and it was the first summer I wasn't going back to Cousins. And that, I minded. That, I mourned. I'd thought I'd be in Cousins every summer of my life. The summer house was the only place I wanted to be. It was the only place I ever wanted to be.

"You're still coming, right?" Taylor asked me.

"Yeah. I told you I was."

Her nose wrinkled. "I know, but—" Taylor's voice broke off. "Never mind."

I knew Taylor was waiting for things to go back to normal again, to be like before. But they could never be like before. I was never going to be like before.

I used to believe. I used to think that if I wanted it bad enough, wished hard enough, everything would work out the way it was supposed to. Destiny, like Susannah said. I wished for Conrad on every birthday, every shooting star, every lost eyelash, every penny in a fountain was dedicated to the one I loved. I thought it would always be that way.

Taylor wanted me to forget about Conrad, to just erase him from my mind and memory. She kept saying things like, "Everybody has to get over a first love, it's a rite of passage." But Conrad wasn't just my first love. He wasn't some rite of passage. He was so much more than that. He and Jeremiah and Susannah were my family. In my memory, the three of them would always be entwined, forever linked. There couldn't be one without the others.

If I forgot Conrad, if I evicted him from my heart, pretended like he was never there, it would be like doing those things to Susannah. And that, I couldn't do.

chapter two

It used to be that the week school let out in June, we'd pack up the car and head straight to Cousins. My mother would go to Costco the day before and buy jugs of apple juice and economy-size boxes of granola bars, sunscreen, and whole grain cereal. When I begged for Lucky Charms or Cap'n Crunch, my mother would say, "Beck will have plenty of cereal that'll rot your teeth out, don't you worry." Of course she'd be right. Susannah—Beck to my mother—loved her kid cereal, just like me. We went through a lot of cereal at the summer house. It never even had a chance to go stale. There was one summer when the boys ate cereal for breakfast, lunch, and dinner. My brother, Steven, was Frosted Flakes, Jeremiah was Cap'n Crunch, and Conrad was Corn Pops. Jeremiah and Conrad were Beck's boys, and they loved their cereal. Me, I ate whatever was left over with sugar on top.

I'd been going to Cousins my whole life. We'd never skipped a summer, not once. Almost seventeen years of me playing catch-up to the boys, of hoping and wishing that one day I would be old enough to be a part of their crew. The summer boys crew. I finally made it, and now it was too late. In the pool, on the last night of the last summer, we said we'd always come back. It's scary how easy promises were broken. Just like that.

When I got home last summer, I waited. August turned into September, school started, and still I waited. It wasn't like Conrad and I had made any declarations. It wasn't like he was my boyfriend. All we'd done was kiss. He was going to college, where there would be a million other girls. Girls without curfews, girls on his hall, all smarter and prettier than me, all mysterious and brand-new in a way that I could never be.

I thought about him constantly—what it all meant, what we were to each other now. Because we couldn't go back. I knew *I* couldn't. What happened between us— between me and Conrad, between me and Jeremiah— it changed everything. And so when August and September began and still the phone didn't ring, all I had to do was think back to the way he'd looked at me that last night, and I knew there was still hope. I knew that I hadn't imagined it all. I couldn't have.

According to my mother, Conrad was all moved into

his dorm room, he had an annoying roommate from New Jersey, and Susannah worried he wasn't getting enough to eat. My mother told me these things casually, offhandedly, so as not to injure my pride. I never pressed her for more information. The thing is, I knew he'd call. I *knew* it. All I had to do was wait.

The call came the second week of September, three weeks since the last time I'd seen him. I was eating strawberry ice cream in the living room, and Steven and I were fighting over the remote control. It was a Monday night, nine p.m., prime TV-watching time. The phone rang, and neither Steven nor I made a move to grab it. Whoever got up would lose the battle for the TV.

My mother picked it up in her office. She brought the phone into the living room and she said, "Belly, it's for you. It's Conrad." Then she winked.

Everything in me went abuzz. I could hear the ocean in my ears. The rush, the roar in my eardrums. It was like a high. It was golden. I had waited, and this was my reward! Being right, being patient, never felt so good.

Steven was the one to break me out of my reverie. Frowning, he said, "Why would Conrad be calling *you*?"

I ignored him and took the phone from my mother. I walked away from Steven, from the remote, from my melting dish of ice cream. None of it mattered.

I made Conrad wait until I was on the staircase before I said anything. I sat down on the steps and I said, "Hey."

I tried to keep the smile off my face; I knew he would hear it over the phone.

"Hey," he said. "What's up?"

"Nothing much."

"So guess what," he said. "My roommate snores even louder than you do."

He called again the next night, and the night after. We talked for hours at a time. When the phone rang, and it was for me and not Steven, he'd been confused at first. "Why does Conrad keep calling you?" he'd demanded.

"Why do you think? He likes me. We like each other."

Steven had nearly gagged. "He's lost his mind," he said, shaking his head.

"Is it so impossible that Conrad Fisher would like me?" I asked him, crossing my arms defiantly.

He didn't even have to think about his answer. "Yes," he said. "It is so impossible."

And honestly, it was.

It was like a dream. Unreal. After all that pining and longing and wishing, years and years of it, whole summers' worth, *he* was calling *me*. He liked talking to me. I made him laugh even when he didn't want to. I understood what he was going through, because I was sort of going through it too. There were only a few people in the world who loved Susannah the way we did. I thought that would be enough.

We became something. Something that was never exactly

defined, but it was something. It was really something.

A few times, he drove the three and a half hours from school to my house. Once, he spent the night because it got so late my mother didn't want him to drive back. Conrad stayed in the guest room, and I lay in my bed awake for hours, thinking about how he was asleep just a few feet away, in *my* house of all places.

If Steven hadn't hung around us like some kind of disease, I know Conrad would have at least tried to kiss me. But with my brother around it was pretty much impossible. Conrad and I would be watching TV, and Steven would plop right down between us. He'd talk to Conrad about stuff I didn't know or care about, like football. One time, after dinner, I asked Conrad if he wanted to go get frozen custard at Brusters, and Steven chimed right in and said, "Sounds good to me." I glared at him, but he just grinned back at me. And then Conrad took my hand, right in front of Steven, and he said, "Let's all go." So we all went, my mother too. I couldn't believe I was going on dates with my mother and my brother in the backseat.

But really, it all just made that one amazing night in December all the sweeter. Conrad and I went back to Cousins, just the two of us. Perfect nights come so rarely, but that one was. Perfect, I mean. It was the kind of night worth waiting for.

I'm glad we had that night.

Because by May, it was all over.

chapter *three*

I left Marcy's house early. I told Taylor it was so I could
rest up for Justin's party that night. It was partly true. I did
want to rest, but I didn't care about the party. As soon as I
got home, I put on my big Cousins T-shirt, filled a water
bottle with grape soda and crushed ice, and I watched TV
until my head hurt.

It was peacefully, blissfully silent. Just the sounds of the
TV and the air conditioning kicking off and on. I had the
house to myself. Steven had a summer job at Best Buy.
He was saving up for a fifty-inch flat screen he'd take to
college with him in the fall. My mother was home, but
she spent all day locked away in her office, catching up
on work, she said.

I understood. If I were her, I'd want to be alone too.

Taylor came over around six, armed with her hot pink

Victoria's Secret makeup bag. She walked into the living room and saw me lying on the couch in my Cousins T-shirt and frowned. "Belly, you haven't even showered yet?"

"I took a shower this morning," I said, not getting up.

"Yeah, and you laid out in the sun all day." She grabbed my arms and I let her lift me into a sitting position. "Hurry up and get into the shower."

I followed her upstairs and she went to my bedroom while I went to the hall bathroom. I took the fastest shower of my life. Left to her own devices, Taylor was a big snoop and would poke around my room like it was hers.

When I came out Taylor was sitting on my floor in front of my mirror. Briskly, she blended bronzer onto her cheeks. "Want me to do your makeup too?"

"No thanks," I told her. "Close your eyes while I put on my clothes, okay?"

She rolled her eyes and then closed them. "Belly, you're such a prude."

"I don't care if I am," I said, putting on my underwear and my bra. Then I put my Cousins T-shirt on again. "Okay, you can look."

Taylor opened her eyes up superwide and she applied her mascara. "I could do your nails," she offered. "I have three new colors."

"Nah, there's no point." I held up my hands. My nails were bitten down to the quick.

Taylor grimaced. "Well, what are you wearing?"

"This," I said, hiding my smile. I pointed down at my Cousins T-shirt. I'd worn it so many times it had tiny holes around the neck and it was soft as a blankie. I wished I could wear it to the party.

"Very funny," she said, shimmying over to my closet on her knees. She stood up and started rifling around, pushing hangers over to the side, like she didn't already know every article of clothing I owned by heart. Usually I didn't mind, but today I felt sort of itchy and bothered by everything.

I told her, "Don't worry about it. I'm just going to wear my cutoffs and a tank top."

"Belly, people get dressed up for Justin's parties. You've never been so you wouldn't know, but you can't just wear your old cutoffs." Taylor pulled out my white sundress. The last time I'd worn it had been last summer, at that party with Cam. Susannah had told me the dress set me off like a picture frame.

I got up and took the dress from Taylor and put it back into my closet. "That's stained," I said. "I'll find something else."

Taylor sat back down in front of the mirror and said, "Well, then wear that black dress with the little flowers. It makes your boobs look amazing."

"It's uncomfortable; it's too tight," I told her.

"Pretty please?"

Sighing, I took it off the hanger and put it on. Sometimes it was easier to just give in with Taylor. We'd been friends, best friends, since we were little kids. We'd been best friends so long it was more like a habit, the kind of thing you didn't really have a say in anymore.

"See, that looks hot." She came over and zipped me up. "Now, let's talk about our plan of action."

"What plan of action?"

"I think you and Cory Wheeler should make out at the party."

"Taylor—"

She lifted her hand. "Just hear me out. Cory's super-nice *and* he's supercute. If he worked on his body and got a little definition, he could be, like, Abercrombie hot."

I snorted. "Please."

"Well, he's at least as cute as C-word." She never called him by his name anymore. Now he was just "you-know-who," or "C-word."

"Taylor, quit pushing me. I can't be over him just because you want me to."

"Can't you at least try?" she wheedled. "Cory could be your rebound. He wouldn't mind."

"If you bring up Cory one more time, I'm not going to the party," I told her, and I meant it. In fact, I kind of hoped she would bring him up again so I'd have an excuse not to go.

Her eyes widened. "Okay, okay. Sorry. My lips are sealed."

Then she grabbed her makeup bag and sat down on the edge of my bed, and I sat down at her feet. She pulled out a comb and sectioned off my hair. She braided quickly, with fast and sure fingers, and when she was done, she pinned the braid over the crown of my head, to the side. Neither of us spoke while she worked until she said, "I love your hair like this. You look sort of Native American, like a Cherokee princess or something."

I started to laugh, but then I stopped myself. Taylor caught my eye in the mirror and said, "It's okay to laugh, you know. It's okay for you to have fun."

"I know," I said, but I didn't.

Before we left I stopped by my mother's office. She was sitting at her desk with folders and stacks of papers. Susannah had made my mother executor of her will, and there was a lot of paperwork involved with that, I guessed. My mother was on the phone with Susannah's lawyer a lot, going over things. She wanted it to go perfect, Beck's last wishes.

Susannah had left both Steven and me some college money. She'd also left me jewelry. A sapphire tennis bracelet I couldn't picture myself ever wearing. A diamond necklace for my wedding day—she'd written that specifically. Opal earrings and an opal ring. Those were my favorite.

"Mom?"

She looked up at me. "Yes?"

"Have you had dinner?" I knew she hadn't. She hadn't left her office since I'd been home.

"I'm not hungry," she said. "If there isn't any food in the fridge, you can call for a pizza if you want."

"I can fix you a sandwich," I offered. I'd gone to the store earlier that week. Steven and I had been taking turns. I doubted she even knew it was Fourth of July weekend.

"No, that's all right. I'll come down and fix myself something later."

"Okay." I hesitated. "Taylor and I are going to a party. I won't be home too late."

Part of me hoped she'd tell me to stay home. Part of me wanted to offer to stay and keep her company, to see if she maybe wanted to see what was on Turner Classic Movies, pop some popcorn.

She'd already gone back to her paperwork. She was chewing on her ballpoint pen. "Sounds good," she said. "Be careful."

I closed the door behind me.

Taylor was waiting for me in the kitchen, texting on her phone. "Let's hurry up and go already."

"Hold on, I just have to do one last thing." I went over to the fridge and pulled out stuff for a turkey sandwich. Mustard, cheese, white bread.

"Belly, there's gonna be food at the party. Don't eat that now."

"It's for my mom," I said.

I made the sandwich, put it on a plate, covered it with plastic wrap, and left it on the counter where she'd see it.

Justin's party was everything Taylor said it would be. Half our class was there, and Justin's parents were nowhere in sight. Tiki lamps lined the yard, and his speakers were practically vibrating, the music was so loud. Girls were dancing already.

There was a big keg and a big red cooler. Justin was manning the grill, flipping steaks and bratwurst. He had a Kiss the Chef apron on.

"As if anybody would make out with him." Taylor sniffed. Taylor had made a play for Justin at the beginning of the year, before she'd settled on her boyfriend, Davis. She and Justin had gone out a few times before he'd blown her off for a senior.

I'd forgotten to put on bug spray, and the mosquitoes were eating me for dinner. I kept bending down to scratch my legs, and I was glad to do it. Glad to have something to do. I was afraid of accidentally making eye contact with Cory. He was hanging out by the pool.

People were drinking beer out of red plastic cups. Taylor got us both wine coolers. Mine was Fuzzy Navel. It was syrupy and it tasted like chemicals. I took two sips before I threw it away.

Then Taylor spotted Davis over by the beer pong table

and she put her finger to her lips and grabbed my hand. We walked up behind him and Taylor slipped her arms around his back. "Gotcha!" she said.

He turned around and they kissed like they hadn't just seen each other a few hours ago. I stood there for a minute, awkwardly holding on to my purse, looking everywhere but at them. His name was actually Ben Davis, but everyone called him Davis. Davis was really cute; he had dimples and green eyes like sea glass. And he was short, which at first Taylor said was a dealbreaker but now claimed not to mind so much. I hated riding to school with them because they held hands the entire time while I sat in the back like the kid. They broke up at least once a month, and they'd only been dating since April. During one breakup, he'd called her, crying, trying to get back together, and Taylor had put him on speaker. I'd felt guilty for listening but at the same time envious and sort of awestruck that he cared that much, enough to cry.

"Pete's gonna go take a piss," Davis said, hooking his arm around Taylor's waist. "Will you stay and be my partner until he comes back?"

She looked over at me and shook her head. She stepped out of his grasp. "I can't leave Belly."

I shot her a look. "Taylor, you don't need to babysit me. You should play."

"Are you sure?"

"Sure, I'm sure."

I walked away before she could argue with me. I said hi to Marcy, to Frankie who I used to ride the bus with in middle school, to Alice who was my best friend in kindergarten, to Simon who I was on yearbook with. I'd known most of these kids my whole life and yet I'd never felt more homesick for Cousins.

Out of the corner of my eye I saw Taylor chatting it up with Cory, and I made a run for it before she could call me over. I grabbed a soda and I made my way over to the trampoline. There was no one on it yet so I kicked off my flip-flops and climbed on. I laid down right in the middle, careful to hold my skirt close to me. The stars were out, little bright diamond flecks in the sky. I gulped down my Coke, burped a few times, looked around to see if anyone had heard me. But no, everyone was back by the house. Then I tried to count stars, which is pretty much as silly as trying to count grains of sand, but I did it anyway because it was something to do. I wondered when I'd be able to sneak away and go back home. We'd taken my car, and Taylor could get a ride home with Davis. Then I wondered if it would look weird if I wrapped up a few hot dogs to take with me for later.

I hadn't thought about Susannah in two hours, at least. Maybe Taylor was right, maybe this was where I was supposed to be. If I kept wishing for Cousins, kept looking back, I would be doomed forever.

As I was thinking this over, Cory Wheeler climbed

up onto the trampoline and made his way to the middle, to where I was. He laid down right next to me and said, "Hey, Conklin."

Since when were Cory and I on a last-name basis? Since never.

And then I went ahead and said, "Hey, Wheeler." I tried not to look at him. I tried to concentrate on counting stars and not on how close he was to me.

Cory propped himself up on one elbow and said, "Having fun?"

"Sure." My stomach was starting to hurt. Running away from Cory was giving me an ulcer.

"Seen any shooting stars yet?"

"Not yet."

Cory smelled like cologne and beer and sweat, and oddly enough, it wasn't a bad combination. The crickets were so loud and the party seemed really far away.

"So, Conklin."

"Yeah?"

"Are you still seeing that guy you brought to prom? The one with the unibrow?"

I smiled. I couldn't help it. "Conrad doesn't have a unibrow. And no. We, um, broke up."

"Cool," he said, and the word hung in the air.

This was one of those fork-in-the-road kind of moments. The night could go either way. If I leaned in just a little to my left, I could kiss him. I could close my eyes and let myself get lost in Cory Wheeler. I could go right on forgetting. Pretending.

But even though Cory was cute, and he was nice, he was no Conrad. Not even close. Cory was simple, he was like a crew cut, all clean lines and everything going in the same direction. Not Conrad. Conrad could turn my insides out with one look, one smile.

Cory reached over and flicked my arm playfully. "So, Conklin . . . maybe we—"

I sat up. I said the first thing I could think of. "Shoot, I've gotta pee. I'll see you later, Cory!"

I scrambled off the trampoline as fast I could, found my flip-flops, and headed back toward the house. I spotted Taylor by the pool and made a beeline for her. "I need to talk to you," I hissed.

I grabbed her hand and pulled her over by the snack table. "Like, five seconds ago, Cory Wheeler almost asked me out."

"And? What did you say?" Taylor's eyes were gleaming, and I hated how smug she looked, like everything was going according to plan.

"I said I had to pee," I told her.

"Belly! Get your butt back over to that trampoline and make out with him!"

"Taylor, would you stop? I told you I wasn't interested in Cory. I saw you talking to him earlier. Did you make him ask me out?"

She gave a little shrug. "Well . . . he's been into you all year and he's been taking his sweet time asking you out. I might have *gently* pushed him in the right direction. You guys looked so cute on the trampoline together."

I shook my head. "I really wish you hadn't done that."

"I was just trying to take your mind off things!"

"Well, I don't need you to do that," I said.

"Yes, you do so."

We stared at each other for a minute. Some days, days like this, I wanted to wring her neck. She was just so bossy all the time. I was getting pretty sick of Taylor pushing me in this direction and that direction, dressing me up like one of her shabbier, less fortunate dolls. It had always been like this with us.

But the thing was, I finally had a real excuse to leave, and I was relieved. I said, "I think I'm gonna go home."

"What are you talking about? We just got here."

"I'm just not in the mood to be here, okay?"

I guess she was getting sick of me too, because she said, "This is starting to get old, Belly. You've been moping around for months. It's not healthy. . . . My mom thinks you should see someone."

"What? You've been talking to your mom about me?" I glared at her. "Tell your mom to save her psychiatric advice for Ellen."

Taylor gasped. "I can't believe you just said that to me."

Their cat, Ellen, had seasonal affective disorder,

according to Taylor's mother. They had her on antide-pressants all winter, and when she was still moody in the spring, they sent Ellen to a cat whisperer. It didn't do any good. In my opinion, Ellen was just plain mean.

I took a breath. "I listened to you cry about Ellen for months, and then Susannah dies and you want me to just make out with Cory and play beer pong and forget about her? Well, I'm sorry, but I can't."

Taylor looked around quickly before she leaned closer and said, "Don't act like Susannah's the only thing you're sad about, Belly. You're sad about Conrad, too, and you know it."

I couldn't believe she said that to me. It stung. It stung because it was true. But it was still a low blow. My father used to call Taylor indomitable. She was. But for better or for worse, Taylor Jewel was a part of me, and I was a part of her.

Not altogether meanly, I said. "We can't all be like you, Taylor."

"You can try," she suggested, smiling a little. "Listen, I'm sorry about the Cory thing. I just want you to be happy."

"I know."

She put her arm around me, and I let her. "It's going to be an amazing summer, you'll see."

"Amazing," I echoed. I wasn't looking for amazing. I just wanted to get by. To keep moving. If I made it through this summer, the next one would be easier. It had to be.

So I stayed a little while longer. I sat on the porch with Davis and Taylor and I watched Cory flirt with a sophomore girl. I ate a hot dog. Then I went home.

At home the sandwich was still on the counter, still wrapped in plastic. I put it in the fridge and I headed upstairs. My mother's bedroom light was on, but I didn't go in to say good night. I went straight to my room and got back into my big Cousins T-shirt and undid my braid, brushed my teeth, and washed my face. Then I got under the covers and lay in bed, just thinking. I thought, *So this is what life is like now.* Without Susannah, without the boys.

It had been two months. I'd survived June. I thought to myself, *I can do this.* I can go to the movies with Taylor and Davis, I can swim in Marcy's pool, maybe I can even go out with Cory Wheeler. If I do those things, it will be all right. Maybe letting myself forget how good it used to be will make things easier.

But when I slept that night, I dreamed of Susannah and the summer house, and even in my sleep I knew exactly how good it used to be. How right it was. And no matter what you do or how hard you try, you can't stop yourself from dreaming.

chapter *four*
JEREMIAH

Seeing your dad cry really messes with your mind. Maybe not for some people. Maybe some people have dads who are cool with crying and are in touch with their emotions. Not my dad. He's not a crier, and he for sure never encouraged us to cry either. But at the hospital, and then at the funeral home, he cried like a lost little kid.

My mom died early in the morning. Everything happened so fast, it took me a minute to catch up and realize it was all really happening. It doesn't hit you right away. But later that night, the first night without her, it was just me and Conrad at the house. The first time we'd been alone in days.

The house was so quiet. Our dad was at the funeral home with Laurel. The relatives were at a hotel. It was just me and Con. All day, people had been in and out of the house, and now it was just us.

We were sitting at the kitchen table. People had sent over all kinds of stuff. Fruit baskets, sandwich platters, a coffee cake. A big tin of butter cookies from Costco.

I tore off a chunk of the coffee cake and stuffed it into my mouth. It was dry. I tore off another chunk and ate that too. "You want some?" I asked Conrad.

"Nah," he said. He was drinking milk. I wondered it if was old. I couldn't remember the last time anybody had been to the store.

"What's happening tomorrow?" I asked. "Is everyone coming over here?"

Conrad shrugged. "Probably," he said. He had a milk mustache.

That was all we said to each other. He went upstairs to his room, and I cleaned up the kitchen. And then I was tired, and I went up too. I thought about going to Conrad's room, because even though we weren't saying anything, it was better when we were together, less lonely. I stood in the hallway for a second, about to knock, and then I heard him crying. Choked sobs. I didn't go inside. I left him alone. I knew that's the way he would want it. I went to my own room and I got into bed. I cried too.

chapter *five*

I wore my old glasses to the funeral, the ones with the red plastic frames. They were like putting on a too-tight coat from a long time ago. They made me dizzy, but I didn't care. Susannah always liked me in those glasses. She said I looked like the smartest girl in the room, the kind of girl who was going somewhere and knew exactly how she was going to get there. I wore my hair halfway up, because that was the way she liked it. She said it showed my face off.

It felt like the right thing to do, to look the way she liked me best. Even though I knew she only said those things to make me feel better, they still felt true. I believed everything Susannah said. I even believed her when she said she'd never leave. I think we all did, even my mother. We were all surprised when it happened, and even when it became inevitable, a fact, we never really believed it. It seemed impossible. Not our Susannah, not Beck. You always hear about people getting better, beating the odds. I was sure Susannah would be one of them. Even if it was only a one in a million chance. She was one in a million.

Things got bad fast. So bad that my mother was shuttling between Susannah's house in Boston and ours, every other weekend at first and then more frequently. She had to take a leave of absence from work. She had a room at Susannah's house.

The call came early in the morning. It was still dark out. It was bad news, of course; bad news is the only kind that really can't wait. As soon as I heard the phone ring, even in my sleep, I knew. Susannah was gone. I lay there in my bed, waiting for my mother to come and tell me. I could hear her moving around in her room, heard the shower running.

When she didn't come, I went to her room. She was packing, her hair still wet. She looked over at me, her eyes tired and empty. "Beck's gone," she said. And that was it.

I could feel my insides sink. My knees too. So I sat on the ground, against the wall, letting it support me. I thought I knew what heartbreak felt like. I thought heartbreak was me, standing alone at the prom. That was nothing. This, this was heartbreak. The pain in your chest, the ache behind your eyes. The knowing that things will never be the same again. It's all relative, I suppose. You think you know love, you think you know real pain, but you don't. You don't know anything.

I'm not sure when I started crying. When I got started, I couldn't stop. I couldn't breathe.

My mother crossed the room and knelt down on the floor with me, hugging me, rocking me back and forth. But she didn't cry. She wasn't even there. She was an upright reed, an empty harbor.

My mother drove up to Boston that same day. The only reason she'd even been at home that day had been to check on me and get a change of clothes. She'd thought there'd be more time. She should've been there, when Susannah died. If only for the boys. I was sure she was thinking the same thoughts.

In her best professor voice, she told Steven and me that we would drive ourselves up in two days, the day of the funeral. She didn't want us in the way of funeral preparations; there was a lot of work to be done. Ends in need of tying up.

My mother had been named executor of the will, and of course Susannah had known exactly what she was doing when she'd picked her. It was true that there was no one better for the job, that they'd been going over things even before Susannah died. But even more than that, my mother was at her best when she was busy, doing things. She did not fall apart, not when she was needed. No, my mother rose to the occasion. I wished that was a gene I'd inherited. Because I was at a loss. I didn't know what to do with myself.

I thought about calling Conrad. I even dialed his number a few times. But I couldn't do it. I didn't know what to say. I was afraid of saying the wrong things, of making things worse. And then I thought about calling Jeremiah. But it was the fear that kept me back. I knew that the moment I called, the moment I said it out loud, it would be true. She would really be gone.

On the drive up, we were mostly quiet. Steven's only suit, the one he'd just worn to prom, was wrapped in plastic and hung in the backseat. I hadn't bothered to hang up my dress. "What will we say to them?" I asked at last.

"I don't know," he admitted. "The only funeral I've ever been to is Aunt Shirle's, and she was really old." I was too young to remember that funeral.

"Where will we stay tonight? Susannah's house?"

"No idea."

"How do you suppose Mr. Fisher's handling it?" I couldn't bring myself to picture Conrad or Jeremiah, not yet.

"Whiskey," was Steven's answer.

After that I stopped asking questions.

We changed into our clothes at a gas station thirty miles from the funeral home. As soon as I saw how neat and pressed Steven's suit was, I regretted not hanging up my dress. Back in the car, I kept smoothing down the skirt with my palms, but it didn't help. My mother had told me that rayon was pointless; I should have listened. I also should have tried it on before I packed it. The last time I wore it was to a reception at my mother's university three years ago, and now it was too small.

We got there early, early enough to find my mother bustling around, arranging flowers and talking to Mr. Browne, the funeral director. As soon as she saw me, she frowned. "You should have ironed that dress, Belly," she said.

I bit my bottom lip to keep from saying something I knew I would regret. "There wasn't any time," I said, even though there had been. There had been plenty of time. I tugged down the skirt so it didn't look so short.

She nodded tersely. "Go find the boys, will you? Belly, talk to Conrad."

Steven and I exchanged a look. What would I say? It had been a month since prom, since we'd last spoken.

We found them in a side room, it had pews and tissue boxes under lacquer covers. Jeremiah's head was bent, like he was praying, something I'd never known him to do. Conrad sat straight, his shoulders squared, staring into nowhere. "Hey," Steven said, clearing his throat. He moved toward them, hugging them roughly.

It occurred to me that I'd never seen Jeremiah in a suit

before. It looked a little too tight; he was uncomfortable, he kept tugging at his neck. But his shoes looked new. I wondered if my mother had helped pick them out.

When it was my turn I hurried over to Jeremiah and hugged him as hard as I could. He felt stiff in my arms. "Thanks for coming," he said, his voice oddly formal.

I had this fleeting thought that maybe he was mad at me, but I pushed it away as quickly as it had come. I felt guilty for even thinking it. This was Susannah's funeral, why would he be thinking about me?

I patted his back awkwardly, my hand moving in small circles. His eyes were impossibly blue, which was what happened when he cried.

"I'm really sorry," I said and immediately regretted saying it, because the words were so ineffectual. They didn't convey what I really meant, how I really felt. "I'm sorry" was just as pointless as rayon.

Then I looked at Conrad. He was sitting back down again, his back stiff, his white shirt one big wrinkle. "Hey," I said, sitting down next to him.

"Hey," he said. I wasn't sure if I should hug him or leave him be. So I squeezed his shoulder, and he didn't say anything. He was made of stone. I made a promise to myself: I would not leave his side all day. I would be right there, I would be a tower of strength, just like my mother.

My mother and Steven and I sat in the fourth pew, behind Conrad and Jeremiah's cousins and Mr. Fisher's brother and his wife, who was wearing too much perfume. I thought my mother should be in the first row, and I told her so, in a whisper. She sneezed and told me it didn't matter. I guessed she was right. Then she took off her suit jacket and draped it over my bare thighs.

I turned around once and saw my father in the back. For some reason, I hadn't expected to see him there. Which was weird, because he'd known Susannah too, so it only made sense that he'd be at her funeral. I gave him a little wave, and he waved back.

"Dad's here," I whispered to my mother.

"Of course he is," she said. She didn't look back.

Jeremiah and Conrad's school friends sat in a bunch together, toward the back. They looked awkward and out of place. The guys kept their heads down and the girls whispered to one another nervously.

The service was long. A preacher I'd never met delivered the eulogy. He said nice things about Susannah. He called her kind, compassionate, graceful, and she was all of those things, but it sounded a lot like he'd never met her. I leaned in close to my mother to tell her so, but she was nodding along with him.

I thought I wouldn't cry again, but I did, a lot. Mr. Fisher got up and thanked everyone for coming, told us we were welcome to come by the house afterward for a reception. His voice broke a few times, but he managed to keep it together. When I last saw him, he was tan and confident and tall. Seeing him that day, he looked like a man who was lost in a snowstorm. Shoulders hunched, face pale. I thought about how hard it must be for him to stand up there, in front of everybody who loved her. He had cheated on her, left her when she needed him most, but in the end, he had shown up. He'd held her hand those last few weeks. Maybe he'd thought there'd be more time too.

It was a closed casket. Susannah told my mother she didn't want everybody gawking at her when she didn't look her best. Dead people looked fake, she explained. Like they were made of wax. I reminded myself that the person inside the coffin wasn't Susannah, that it didn't matter what she looked like because she was already gone.

When it was over, after we'd said the Lord's Prayer, we formed our processional, everybody taking their turn to offer condolences. I felt strangely adult there, standing with my mother and my brother. Mr. Fisher leaned down and gave me a stiff hug, his eyes wet. He shook Steven's hand and when he hugged my mother, she whispered something in his ear and he nodded.

When I hugged Jeremiah, we were both crying so hard, we were holding each other up. His shoulders kept shaking.

When I hugged Conrad, I wanted to say something, to comfort him. Something better than "I'm sorry." But it was over so quick, there wasn't any time to say more than that. I had a whole line of people behind me, all waiting to pay their condolences too.

The cemetery wasn't very far. My heels kept sticking in the ground. It must have rained the day before. Before they lowered Susannah into the wet ground, Conrad and Jeremiah both put a white rose on top of the coffin, and then the rest of us added more flowers. I picked a pink peony. Someone sang a hymn. When it was over, Jeremiah didn't move. He stood right where her grave was going to be, and he cried. It was my mother who went to him. She took him by the hand, and she spoke to him softly.

Back at Susannah's house, Jeremiah and Steven and I slipped away to Jeremiah's bedroom. We sat on his bed in our fancy clothes. "Where's Conrad?" I said. I hadn't forgotten my vow to stay by his side, but he was making it hard, the way he kept disappearing.

"Let's leave him alone for a while," Jeremiah said. "Are you guys hungry?"

I was, but I didn't want to say so. "Are you?"

"Yeah, sort of. There's food downstairs." His voice lingered on the word "downstairs." I knew he didn't want to go down there and face all those people, have to see the pity in their eyes. *How sad*, they'd say, *look at those two young boys she left behind.* His friends hadn't come to the house; they'd left right after the burial. It was all adults down there.

"I'll go," I offered.

"Thanks," he said gratefully.

I got up and shut the door behind me. In the hallway I stopped to look at their family portraits. They were matted and framed in black, all the same kind of frame. In one picture, Conrad was wearing a bow tie and he was missing his front teeth. In another, Jeremiah was eight or nine and he had on the Red Sox cap he refused to take off for, like, a whole summer. He said it was a lucky hat; he wore it every day for three months. Every couple of weeks, Susannah would wash it and then put it back in his room while he slept.

Downstairs the adults were milling around, drinking coffee and talking in hushed voices. My mother stood at the buffet table, cutting cake for strangers. They were strangers to me, anyway. I wondered if she knew them, if they knew who she was to Susannah, how she was her best friend, how they'd spent every summer together for almost their whole lives.

I grabbed two plates and my mother helped me load them up. "Are you guys all right upstairs?" she asked me, putting a wedge of blue cheese on the plate.

I nodded and slid it right back off. "Jeremiah doesn't like blue cheese," I told her. Then I took a handful of water crackers and a cluster of green grapes. "Have you seen Conrad?"

"I think he's in the basement," she said. Rearranging

the cheese plate, she added, "Why don't you go check on him and bring him a plate? I'll take this one up to the boys."

"Okay." I picked up the plate and crossed the dining room just as Jeremiah and Steven came downstairs. I stood there and watched Jeremiah stop and talk to people, letting them hug him and grasp his hand. Our eyes met, and I lifted my hand and waved it just barely. He lifted his and did the same, rolling his eyes a little at the woman clutching his arm. Susannah would have been proud.

Then I headed downstairs, to the basement. The basement was carpeted and soundproofed. Susannah had it set up when Conrad took up the electric guitar.

It was dark; Conrad hadn't turned the lights on. I waited for my eyes to adjust, and then I crept down the stairs, feeling my way.

I found him soon enough. He was lying down on the couch with his head in a girl's lap. She was running her hands along the top of his head, like they belonged there. Even though summer had just barely started, she was tan. Her shoes were off, her bare legs were stretched out on top of the coffee table. And Conrad, he was stroking her leg.

Everything in me seized up, pulled in tight.

I had seen her at the funeral. I'd thought she was really pretty, and I'd wondered who she was. She looked South Asian, like she might be Indian. She had dark hair and dark eyes and she was wearing a black miniskirt and a white and black polka-dot blouse. And a headband, she was wearing a black headband.

She saw me first. "Hey," she said.

That's when Conrad looked over and saw me standing in the doorway with a plate of cheese and crackers. He sat up. "Is that food for us?" he asked, not quite looking at me.

"My mother sent it," I said, and my voice came out mumbly and quiet. I walked over and put the plate on the coffee table. I stood there for a second, unsure of what to do next.

"Thanks," the girl said, in a way that sounded more like, *You can go now.* Not in a mean way, but in a way that made it clear I was interrupting.

I backed out of the room slowly but when I got to the stairs, I started to run. I ran by all the people in the living room and I could hear Conrad coming after me.

"Wait a minute," he called out.

I'd almost made it through the foyer when he caught up to me and grabbed my arm.

"What do you want?" I said, shaking him off. "Let go of me."

"That was Aubrey," he said, letting go.

Aubrey, the girl who broke Conrad's heart. I'd pictured her differently. I'd pictured her blond. This girl was prettier than what I had pictured. I could never compete with a girl like that.

I said, "Sorry I interrupted your little moment."

"Oh, grow up," he said.

There are moments in life that you wish with all your heart you could take back. Like, just erase from existence. Like, if you could, you'd erase yourself right out of existence too, just to make that moment not exist.

What I said next was one of those moments for me.

On the day of his mother's funeral, to the boy I loved more than I had ever loved anything or anyone, I said, "Go to hell."

It was the worst thing I've ever said to anyone, ever. It wasn't that I'd never said the words before. But the look on his face. I'll never forget it. The look on his face made me want to die. It confirmed every mean and low thing I'd ever thought about myself, the stuff you hope and pray no one will ever know about you. Because if they knew, they would see the real you, and they would despise you.

Conrad said, "I should have known you'd be like this."

Miserably, I asked him, "What do you mean?"

He shrugged, his jaw tight. "Forget it."

"No, say it."

He started to turn around, to leave, but I stopped him. I stood in his way. "Tell me," I said, my voice rising.

He looked at me and said, "I knew it was a bad idea, starting something with you. You're just a kid. It was a huge mistake."

"I don't believe you," I said.

People were starting to look. My mother was standing

in the living room, talking to people I didn't recognize. She'd glanced up when I'd started speaking. I couldn't even look at her; I could feel my face burning.

I knew the right thing to do was to walk away. I knew that was what I was supposed to do. In that moment, it was like I was floating above myself and I could see me and how everybody in that room was looking at me. But when Conrad just shrugged and started to leave again, I felt so mad, and so—small. I wanted to stop myself, but I couldn't quit.

"I hate you," I said.

Conrad turned around and nodded, like he'd expected me to say exactly that. "Good," he said. The way he looked at me then, pitying and fed up and just over it. It made me feel sick.

"I never want to see you again," I said, and then I pushed past him, and I ran up the staircase so fast I tripped on the top step. I fell right onto my knees, hard. I think I heard someone gasp. I could barely see through my tears. Blindly, I got back up and ran to the guest room.

I took off my glasses and lay down on the bed and cried.

It wasn't Conrad I hated. It was myself.

My father came up after a while. He knocked a few times, and when I didn't answer, he came in and sat on the edge of the bed.

"Are you all right?" he asked me. His voice was so gentle, I could feel tears leaking out of the corners of my eyes again. No one should be nice to me. I didn't deserve it.

I rolled away so my back was to him. "Is Mom mad at me?"

"No, of course not," he said. "Come back downstairs and say good-bye to everyone."

"I can't." How could I go back downstairs and face everyone after I'd made that scene? It was impossible. I was humiliated, and I had done it to myself.

"What happened with you and Conrad, Belly? Did you have a fight? Did you two break up?" It was so odd to hear the words "break up" come out of my dad's mouth. I couldn't discuss it with him. It was just too bizarre.

"Dad, I can't talk about this stuff with you. Could you just go? I want to be alone."

"All right," he said, and I could hear the hurt in his voice. "Do you want me to get your mother?"

She was the last person I wanted to see. Right away, I said, "No, please don't."

The bed creaked as my father got up and closed the door.

The only person I wanted was Susannah. She was the only one. And then I had a thought, clear as day. I would never be somebody's favorite again. I would never be a kid again, not in the same way. That was all over now. She was really gone.

I hoped Conrad listened to me. I hoped I never saw him again. If I ever had to look at him again, if he looked at me the way he did that day, it would break me.

chapter *six*
JULY 3

When the phone rang early the next morning, my first thought was, *The only kind of calls you get this early in the morning are the bad ones.* I was right, sort of.

I think I was still in a dream state when I heard his voice. For one long second, I thought it was Conrad, and for that second, I could not catch my breath. Conrad calling me again—that was enough to make me forget how to breathe. But it wasn't Conrad. It was Jeremiah.

They were brothers, after all; their voices were alike. Alike but not the same. He, Jeremiah, said, "Belly, it's Jeremiah. Conrad's gone."

"What do you mean 'gone'?" Suddenly I was wide awake and my heart was in my throat. Gone had come to mean something different, in a way that it hadn't used to. Something permanent.

"He took off from summer school a couple of days ago and he hasn't come back. Do you know where he is?"

"No." Conrad and I hadn't spoken since Susannah's funeral.

"He missed two exams. He'd never do that." Jeremiah sounded desperate, panicky even. I'd never heard him sound that way. He was always at ease, always laughing, never serious. And he was right, Conrad would never do that, he'd never just leave without telling anybody. Not the old Conrad, anyway. Not the Conrad I had loved since I was ten years old, not him.

I sat up, rubbed at my eyes. "Does your dad know?"

"Yeah. He's freaking out. He can't deal with this kind of thing." This kind of thing would be Susannah's domain, not Mr. Fisher's.

"What do you want to do, Jere?" I tried to make my voice sound the way my mother's would. Calm, reasonable. Like I wasn't scared out of my mind, the thought of Conrad gone. It wasn't so much that I thought he was in trouble. It was that if he left, really left, he might never come back. And that scared me more than I could say.

"I don't know." Jeremiah let out a big gust of air. "His phone has been off for days. Do you think you could help me find him?"

Immediately I said, "Yes. Of course. Of course I can."

Everything made sense in that moment. This was my chance to make things right with Conrad. The way I saw it, this was what I had been waiting for and I hadn't even known it. It was like the last two months I had been sleepwalking, and now here I was, finally awake. I had a goal, a purpose.

That last day I'd said horrible things. Unforgiveable things. Maybe, if I helped him in some small way, I'd be able to fix what was broken.

Even so, as scared as I was at the thought of Conrad being gone, as eager as I was to redeem myself, the thought of being near him again terrified me. No one on this earth affected me the way Conrad Fisher did.

As soon as Jeremiah and I got off the phone, I was everywhere at once, throwing underwear and T-shirts into my big overnight bag. How long would it take us to find him? Was he okay? I would have known if he wasn't okay, wouldn't I? I packed my toothbrush, a comb. Contact solution.

My mother was ironing clothes in the kitchen. She was staring off into nowhere, her forehead one big crease. "Mom?" I asked.

Startled, she looked at me. "What? What's up?"

I'd already planned what I'd say next. "Taylor's having some kind of breakdown because she and Davis broke up again. I'm gonna stay over at her place tonight, maybe tomorrow, too, depending on how she feels."

I held my breath, waiting for her to speak. My mother has a bullshit detector like no one I've ever known. It's more than a mother's intuition, it's like a homing device. But no alerts went off, no bells or whistles. Her face was perfectly blank.

"All right," she said, going back to her ironing.

And then, "Try and be home tomorrow night," she said. "I'll make halibut." She spritzed starch on khaki pants. I was home free. I should have felt relieved, but I didn't, not really.

"I'll try," I said.

For a moment, I thought about telling her the truth. Of all people, she'd understand. She'd want to help. She loved them both. It was my mother who took Conrad to the emergency room the time he broke his arm skateboarding, because Susannah was shaking so hard she couldn't drive. My mother was steady, solid. She always knew what to do.

Or at least, she used to. Now I wasn't so sure. When Susannah got sick again, my mother went on autopilot, doing what needed doing. Barely present. The other day I'd come downstairs to find her sweeping the front hallway, and her eyes were red, and I'd been afraid. She wasn't the crying kind. Seeing her like that, like an actual person and not just my mother, it almost made me not trust her.

My mother set down her iron. She picked up her purse from the counter and pulled out her wallet. "Buy Taylor some Ben & Jerry's, on me," she said, handing me a twenty.

"Thanks, Mom," I said, taking the twenty and stuffing it into my pocket. It would come in handy for gas money later.

"Have fun," she said, and she was gone again. Absent. Ironing the same pair of khaki pants she'd just gone over.

When I was in my car, driving away, I finally let myself feel it. Relief. No silent, sad mother, not today. I hated to leave her and I hated to be near her, because she made me remember what I wanted most to forget. Susannah was gone, and she wasn't coming back, and none of us would be the same ever again.

chapter *seven*

At Taylor's house, the front door was almost never locked. Her staircase, with its long banister and shiny wooden steps, was as familiar to me as my own.

After I let myself into the house, I went straight up to her room.

Taylor was lying on her stomach, flipping through gossip magazines. As soon as she saw me, she sat up and said, "Are you a masochist, or what?"

I threw my duffel bag on the floor and sat down next to her. I'd called her on the way over; I'd told her everything. I hadn't wanted to, but I'd done it.

"Why are you going off looking for him?" she demanded. "He's not your boyfriend anymore."

I sighed. "Like he ever really was."

"My point exactly." She thumbed through a magazine

and handed it to me. "Check it out. I could see you in this bikini. The white bandeau one. It'll look hot with your tan."

"Jeremiah's going to be here soon," I said, looking at the magazine and handing it back to her. I couldn't picture me in that bikini. But I could picture her in it.

"You *so* should have picked Jeremy," she said. "Conrad is basically a crazy person."

I'd told her and told her how it wasn't as easy as picking one or the other. Nothing ever was. It wasn't as though I'd even had a choice, not really.

"Conrad's not crazy, Taylor." She'd never forgiven Conrad for not liking her the summer I brought her to Cousins, the summer we were fourteen. Taylor was used to all the boys liking her, she was unaccustomed to being ignored. Which was exactly what Conrad had done. Not Jeremiah, though. As soon as she batted her big brown eyes at him, he was hers. Her *Jeremy*, that's what she'd called him—in that teasing kind of way, the kind that boys love. Jeremiah lapped it right up, too, until she ditched him for my brother, Steven.

Pursing her lips, Taylor said, "Fine, maybe that was a *little* harsh. Maybe he's not crazy. But, like, what? Are you always just going to be sitting around waiting for him? Whenever he wants?"

"No! But he's in some kind of trouble. He needs his friends now more than ever," I said, picking at a loose strand on the carpet. "No matter what happened between us, we'll always be friends."

She rolled her eyes. "Whatever. The only reason I'm even signing off on this is for you to get closure."

"Closure?"

"Yes. I can see now that it's the only way. You need to see Conrad face-to-face and tell him you're over him and you're not gonna play his games anymore. Then and only then can you move on from his lame ass."

"Taylor, I'm not innocent in all this either." I swallowed. "The last time I saw him, I was awful."

"Whatever. The point is, you need to move on. On to greener pastures." She eyed me. "Like Cory. Who, by the way, I doubt you even have a chance with anymore after last night."

Last night seemed like a thousand years ago. I did my best to look contrite and said, "Hey, thanks again for letting me leave my car here. If my mom calls—"

"Please, Belly. Show a little respect. I'm the queen of lying to parents, unlike you." She sniffed. "You're gonna be back in time for tomorrow night, right? We're all gonna go out on Davis's parents' boat, remember? You promised."

"That's not until eight or nine. I'm sure I'll be back by then. Besides," I pointed out, "I never *promised* you anything."

"Then promise now," she commanded. "Promise you'll be here."

I rolled my eyes. "Why do you want me back here so bad? So you can sic Cory Wheeler on me again? You don't need me. You have Davis."

"I do so need you, even if you are a terrible best friend. Boyfriends aren't the same as best friends and you know it. Pretty soon we'll be in college, you know. What if we go to different schools? What then?" Taylor glared at me, her eyes accusing.

"Okay, okay. I promise." Taylor still had her heart set on us going to the same school, the way we'd always said we would.

She held out her hand to me and we hooked pinkies.

"Is that what you're wearing?" Taylor asked me suddenly.

Looking down at my gray camisole, I said, "Well, yeah."

She shook her head so fast her blond hair swished all around. "Is that what you're wearing to see Conrad *for the first time?*"

"This isn't a date I'm going on, Taylor."

"When you see an ex, you have to look better than you've ever looked. It's, like, the first rule of breakups. You have to make him think, 'Damn, I missed out on *that?*' It's the only way."

I hadn't thought of that. "I don't care what he thinks," I told her.

She was already rifling through my overnight bag. "All you have in here is underwear and a T-shirt. And this old tank top. Ugh. I hate this tank top. It needs to be officially retired."

"Quit it," I said. "Don't go through my stuff."

Taylor leaped up, her face all glowy and excited. "Oh, please let me pack for you, Belly! Please, it would make me so happy."

"No," I said, as firmly as I could. With Taylor, you had to be firm. "I'll probably be back tomorrow. I don't need anything else."

Taylor ignored me and disappeared into her walk-in closet.

My phone rang then, and it was Jeremiah. Before I answered it, I said, "I'm serious, Tay."

"Don't worry, I've got it all covered. Just think of me as your fairy godmother," she said from inside the closet.

I popped open my phone. "Hey," I said. "Where are you?"

"I'm pretty close. About an hour away. Are you at Taylor's?"

"Yeah," I said. "Do you need me to give you the directions again?"

"No, I've got it." He paused, and for a second I thought he'd already hung up. Then he said, "Thanks for doing this."

"Come on," I said.

I thought about saying something else, like how he was one of my best friends and how part of me was almost glad to have a reason to see him again. It just wouldn't be summer without Beck's boys.

But I couldn't get the words to sound right in my head, and before I could figure them out, he hung up.

When Taylor finally emerged from the closet, she was zipping up my bag. "All set," she said, dimpling.

"Taylor—" I tried to grab the bag from her.

"No, just wait until you get wherever you're going. You'll thank me," she said. "I was *very* generous, even though you're totally deserting me."

I ignored the last bit and said, "Thanks, Tay."

"You're welcome," she said, checking out her hair in her bureau mirror. "See how much you need me?" Taylor faced me, her hands on her hips. "How are you guys even planning on finding Conrad, anyway? For all you know, he's under a bridge somewhere."

I hadn't given that part, the actual details, much thought. "I'm sure Jeremiah has some ideas," I said.

Jeremiah showed up in an hour, just like he said he would. We watched from the living room window when his car pulled into Taylor's circular driveway. "Oh my God, he looks so cute," Taylor said, running over to the dresser and putting on lip gloss. "Why didn't you tell me how cute he got?"

The last time she'd seen Jeremiah, he'd been a head shorter and scrawny. It was no wonder she'd gone after Steven instead. But he just looked like Jeremiah to me.

I picked up my bag and headed outside, with Taylor right on my heels.

When I opened the front door, Jeremiah was standing on the front steps. He was wearing his Red Sox cap, and his hair was shorter than the last time I'd seen him. It was strange to see him there, on Taylor's doorstep. Surreal.

"I was just about to call you," he said, taking off his hat. He was a boy unafraid of hat hair, of looking stupid. It was one of his most endearing qualities, one I admired because I pretty much lived in constant fear of embarrassing myself.

I wanted to hug him, but for some reason—maybe because he didn't reach for me first, maybe because I felt shy all of a sudden—I held back. Instead, I said, "You got here really fast."

"I sped like crazy," he said, and then, "Hey, Taylor."

She got on her tiptoes and hugged him and I regretted not hugging him too.

When she stepped away, Taylor surveyed him approvingly and said, "Jeremy, you look good." She smiled at him, waiting for him to tell her she looked good too. When he didn't, she said, "That was your cue to tell me how good I look. Duh."

Jeremiah laughed. "Same old Taylor. You know you look good. You don't need me to tell you."

The two of them smirked at each other.

"We'd better get going," I said.

He took my overnight bag off my shoulder and we followed him to the car. While he made room for my bag in the trunk, Taylor grabbed me by the elbow and said, "Call me when you get wherever you're going, Cinderbelly." She used to call me that when we were little, when we were obsessed with *Cinderella*. She'd sing it right along with the mice. *Cinderbelly, Cinderbelly*.

I felt a sudden rush of affection for her. Nostalgia, a shared history, counted for a lot. More than I'd realized. I'd miss her next year, when the two of us were at different colleges. "Thanks for letting me leave my car here, Tay."

She nodded. Then she mouthed the word *CLOSURE*.

"Bye, Taylor," Jeremiah said, getting into the car.

I got in too. His car was a mess, like always. There were empty water bottles all over the floor and backseat. "Bye," I called out as we began to drive away.

She stood there and waved and watched us. She called back, "Don't forget your promise, Belly!"

"What'd you promise?" Jeremiah asked me, looking in the rearview mirror.

"I promised her I'd be back in time for her boyfriend's Fourth of July party. It's going to be on a boat."

Jeremiah nodded. "You'll be back in time, don't worry. Hopefully I'll have you back by tonight."

"Oh," I said. "Okay."

I guessed I wouldn't need that overnight bag after all. Then he said, "Taylor looks exactly the same."

"Yeah, I guess she does."

And then neither of us said anything. We were just silent.

chapter *eight*
JEREMIAH

I can pinpoint the exact moment everything changed. It was last summer. Con and I were sitting on the porch, and I was trying to talk to him about what a dick the new assistant football coach was.

"Just stick it out," he said.

Easy for him to say. He'd quit. "You don't get it, this guy's crazy," I started to tell him, but he wasn't listening anymore. Their car had just pulled into the driveway. Steven got out first, then Laurel. She asked where my mom was and gave me a big hug. She hugged Conrad next and I started to say, "Hey, where's the Belly Button?" And there she was.

Conrad saw her first. He was looking over Laurel's shoulder. At her. She walked toward us. Her hair was swinging around all over the place and her legs looked miles long. She was wearing cutoffs and dirty sneakers. Her bra strap was sticking out of her tank top. I swear I never noticed her bra strap before. She had a funny look on her face, a look I didn't recognize. Like shy and nervous, but proud at the same time.

I watched Conrad hug her, waiting my turn. I wanted to ask her what she'd been thinking about, why she had that look on her face. I didn't do it though. I stepped around Conrad and grabbed her up and said something stupid. It made her laugh, and then she was just Belly again. And that was a relief, because I didn't want her to be anything but just Belly.

I'd known her my whole life. I'd never thought of her as a girl. She was one of us. She was my friend. Seeing her in a different way, even just for a second, it shook me up.

My dad used to say that with everything in life, there's the game-changing moment. The one moment everything else hinges upon, but you hardly ever know it at the time. The three-pointer early on in the second quarter that changes up the whole tempo of the game. Wakes people up, brings them back to life. It all goes back to that one moment.

I might have forgotten about it, that moment when their car drove up and this girl walked out, a girl I barely recognized. It could have just been one of those things. You know, where a person catches your eye, like a whiff of perfume when you walk down the street. You keep walking. You forget. I might have forgotten. Things might have gone back to the way they were before.

But then came the game-changing moment.

It was nighttime, maybe a week into the summer. Belly and I were hanging out by the pool, and she was cracking up over something I said, I don't remember what. I loved that I could make her laugh. Even though she laughed a lot and it wasn't some kind of feat, it felt great. She said, "Jere, you're, like, the funniest person I know."

It was one of the best compliments of my life. But that wasn't the game-changing moment.

That happened next. I was really on a roll, doing an impersonation of Conrad when he wakes up in the mornings. A whole Frankenstein sort of thing. Then Conrad came out and sat next to her on the deck chair. He pulled on her ponytail and said, "What's so funny?"

Belly looked up at him, and she was actually blushing. Her face was all flushed, and her eyes were shining. "I don't remember," she said.

My gut just twisted. I felt like somebody had drop-kicked me in the stomach. I was jealous, crazy jealous. Of Conrad. And when she got up a little while later to get a soda, I watched him watch her walk away and I felt sick inside.

That was when I knew things would never be the same.

I wanted to tell Conrad that he had no right. That he'd ignored her all these years, that he couldn't just decide to take her just because he felt like it.

She was all of ours. My mom adored her. She called Belly her secret daughter. She looked forward to seeing her all year. Steven, even though he gave her a hard time, he was really protective of her. Everyone took care of Belly, she just didn't know it. She was too busy looking at Conrad. For as long as any of us could remember, she had loved Conrad.

All I knew was, I wanted her to look at me like that. After that day, I was done for. I liked her, as more than a friend. I maybe even loved her.

There have been other girls. But they weren't her.

I didn't want to call Belly for help. I was pissed at her. It wasn't just that she'd picked Conrad. That was old news. She was always going to pick Conrad. But we were friends too. How many times had she called me since my mom died? Twice? A few texts and emails?

But sitting in the car next to her, smelling her Belly Conklin smell (Ivory soap and coconuts and sugar), the way her nose wrinkled up as she thought, her nervous smile and chewed-up fingernails. The way she said my name.

When she leaned forward to mess with the AC vents, her hair brushed against my leg and it was really soft. It made me remember all over again. It made it hard to stay pissed and keep her at arm's length the way I'd planned. It was pretty damn near impossible. When I was near her, I just wanted to grab her and hold her and kiss the shit out of her. Maybe then she'd finally forget about my asshole of a brother.

chapter *nine*

"So where are we going?" I asked Jeremiah. I tried to catch his eye, to make him look at me, just for a second. It seemed like he hadn't looked me in the eye once since he's showed up, and it made me nervous. I needed to know that things were okay between us.

"I don't know," he said. "I haven't talked to Con in a while. I have no clue where he'd go. I was hoping you'd have some ideas."

The thing was, I didn't. Not really. Not at all, actually. I cleared my throat. "Conrad and I haven't spoken since—since May."

Jeremiah looked at me sideways, but he didn't say anything. I wondered what Conrad had told him. Probably not much.

I kept talking because he wasn't. "Have you called his roommate?"

"I don't have his number. I don't even know his name."

"His name is Eric," I said quickly. I was glad to know that at least. "It's his same roommate from the school year. They stayed in the same room for summer school. So, um, I guess that's where we'll go, then. To Brown. We'll talk to Eric, to people on his hall. You never know, he could just be hanging out on campus."

"Sounds like a plan." As he checked his rearview mirror and changed lanes, he asked me, "So you've been to visit Con at school?"

"No," I said, looking out the window. It was a pretty embarrassing thing to admit. "Have you?"

"My dad and I helped him move into the dorms." Almost reluctantly he added, "Thanks for coming."

"Sure," I said.

"So Laurel's cool with it?"

"Oh, yeah, totally," I lied. "I'm glad I could come."

I used to look forward to seeing Conrad all year. I used to wish for summer the way kids wished for Christmas. It was all I thought about. Even now, even after everything, he was still all I thought about.

Later I turned on the radio to fill the silence between Jeremiah and me.

Once I thought I heard him start to say something, and I said, "Did you just say something?"

He said, "Nope."

For a while we just drove. Jeremiah and me were two

people who never ran out of things to say to each other, but there we were, not saying a word.

Finally he said, "I saw Nona last week. I stopped by the retirement home she's been working at."

Nona was Susannah's hospice nurse. I'd met her a few times. She was funny, and strong. Nona was slight, maybe five foot two with spindly arms and legs, but I'd seen her haul up Susannah like she weighed nothing. Which, toward the end, I guess she very nearly did.

chapter *ten*

When Susannah got really sick again, no one told me right away. Not Conrad, or my mother, or Susannah herself. It all happened so fast.

I tried getting out of going to see Susannah that last time. I told my mother I had a trig exam that counted for a quarter of my grade. I would have said anything to get out of going. "I'm going to have to study all weekend. I can't come. Maybe next weekend," I said over the phone. I tried to make my voice casual and not desperate. "Okay?"

Immediately she said, "No. Not okay. You're coming up this weekend. Susannah wants to see you."

"But—"

"No buts." Her voice was razor sharp. "I already bought your train ticket. See you tomorrow."

On the train ride up, I worked hard to come up with things I could say when I saw Susannah. I would tell her about how hard trig was, how Taylor was in love, how I was thinking of running for class secretary, which was a lie. I wasn't going to run for class secretary, but I knew that Susannah would like the sound of it. I would tell her all of those things, and I would not ask about Conrad.

My mother picked me up at the train station. When I got into the car, she said, "I'm glad you came."

She went on to say, "Don't worry, Conrad's not here."

I didn't answer her, I just stared out the window. I was unjustifiably mad at her for making me come. Not that she cared. She kept right on talking. "I'm going to go ahead and warn you that she doesn't look good. She's tired. She's very tired, but she's excited to see you."

As soon as she said the words, "she doesn't look good," I closed my eyes. I hated myself for being afraid to see her, for not visiting more often. But I wasn't like my mother, as strong and durable as steel. Seeing Susannah like that, it was too hard. It felt like pieces of her, of who she used to be, crumpled away every time. Seeing her like that made it real.

When we pulled into the driveway, Nona was outside smoking a cigarette. I'd met Nona a couple of weeks before, when Susannah first moved back home. Nona had a very intimidating handshake. When we stepped out of the car, she was Purelling her hands and spraying Febreze on her uniform like she was a teenager smoking in secret, even though Susannah didn't mind it; she loved cigarettes once in a while but couldn't smoke them anymore. Just pot, just once in a while.

"Morning," Nona called out, waving to us.

"Morning," we called back.

She was sitting on the front porch. "Nice to see you," she said to me. To my mother, she said, "Susannah's all dressed and waiting for you two downstairs."

My mother sat down next to Nona. "Belly, you go on in first. I'm going to chat with Nona." And by "chat," I knew she meant she too was going to have a cigarette. She and Nona had gotten to be pretty friendly.

Nona was pragmatic and also intensely spiritual. She invited my mother to go to church with her once, and even though my mother was not religious in the least, she went. At first I thought it was just to humor Nona, but then when she started going to church alone back home, I realized it was more than that. She was looking for some kind of peace.

I said, "By myself?" and I regretted it right away. I didn't want either of them to judge me for being afraid. I was already judging myself.

"She's waiting for you," my mother said.

Which she was. She was sitting in the living room, and she was wearing actual clothes and not her pajamas. She had on makeup. Her peachy blush was bright and garish against her chalky skin. She'd made an effort, for me. So as not to scare me. So I pretended not to be scared.

"My favorite girl," she said, opening her arms for me.

I hugged her, carefully as I could, I told her she looked so much better. I lied.

She said Jeremiah wouldn't be home until later that night, that us girls had the house all to ourselves for the afternoon.

My mother came inside then, but left the two of us alone. She came into the living room to say a quick hello and then she fixed lunch while we caught up.

As soon as my mother left the room, Susannah said, "If you're worried about running into Conrad, don't be, sweetie. He won't be here this weekend."

I swallowed. "Did he tell you?"

She half laughed. "That boy doesn't tell me anything. Your mother mentioned that prom didn't go . . . as well as we'd hoped. I'm sorry, honey."

"He broke up with me," I told her. It was more complicated than that, but when you boiled it all down, that was what had happened. It had happened because he'd wanted it to. It had always been his call—his decision whether or not we were together.

Susannah took my hand and held it. "Don't hate Conrad," she said.

"I don't," I lied. I hated him more than anything. I

loved him more than anything. Because, he *was* everything. And I hated that, too.

"Connie's having a hard time with all of this. It's a lot." She paused and pushed my hair out of my face, her hand lingering on my forehead as if I had a fever. As if I was the one who was sick, in need of comfort. "Don't let him push you away. He needs you. He loves you, you know."

I shook my head. "No, he doesn't." In my head, I added, *The only person he loves is himself. And you.*

She acted like she hadn't heard me. "Do you love him?"

When I didn't answer, she nodded as if I had. "Will you do something for me?"

Slowly, I nodded.

"Look after him for me. Will you do that?"

"You won't need me to look after him, Susannah, you'll be here to do it," I said, and I tried not to sound desperate, but it didn't matter.

Susannah smiled and said, "You're my girl, Belly."

After lunch, Susannah took a nap. She didn't wake up until late afternoon, and when she did, she was irritable and disoriented. She snapped at my mother once, which terrified me. Susannah never snapped at anybody. Nona tried to put her to bed, and at first Susannah refused, but then she gave in. On the way to her bedroom, she gave me a little halfhearted wink.

Jeremiah came home around dinnertime. I was relieved

to see him. He made everything lighter, easier. Just seeing his face took away some of the strain of being there.

He walked into the kitchen and said, "What's that burning smell? Oh, Laurel's cooking. Hey, Laurel!"

My mother swatted at him with a kitchen towel. He dodged her and started looking under pan covers playfully.

"Hey, Jere," I said to him. I was sitting on a stool, shelling beans.

He looked over at me and said, "Oh, hey. How are you?" Then he walked over to me and gave me a quick half hug. I tried to search his eyes for some clue as to how he was doing, but he didn't let me. He kept moving around, joking with Nona and my mother.

In some ways, he was the same Jeremiah, but in other ways, I could see how this had changed him. Had aged him. Everything took more effort, his jokes, his smiles. Nothing was easy anymore.

chapter *eleven*

It felt like forever before Jeremiah spoke again. I was pretending to be asleep, and he was drumming his fingers along the steering wheel. Suddenly he said, "This was my prom's theme song."

Right away I opened my eyes and asked, "How many proms have you been to?"

"Total? Five."

"What? Yeah, right. I don't believe you," I said, even though I did. Of course Jeremiah had been to five proms. He was exactly that guy, the one everyone wanted to go with. He would know how to make a girl feel like the prom queen even if she was nobody.

Jeremiah starting ticking off with his fingers. "Junior year, I went to two, mine and Flora Martinez's at Sacred

Heart. This year, I went to my prom and two others. Sophia Franklin at—"

"Okay, okay. I get it. You're in demand." I leaned forward and fiddled with the air conditioner control.

"I had to buy a tux because it was cheaper than renting over and over again," he said. Jeremiah looked straight ahead, and then he said the last thing I was expecting him to say. "You looked good at yours. I liked your dress."

I stared at him. Did Conrad show him our pictures? Had he told him anything? "How do you know?"

"My mom got one of the pictures framed."

I hadn't expected him to bring up Susannah. I'd thought prom would be a safe subject. I said, "I heard you were prom king at your prom."

"Yeah."

"I bet that was fun."

"Yeah, it was pretty fun."

I should have brought Jeremiah instead. If it had been Jeremiah, things would have been different. He would have said all the right things. It would have been Jeremiah in the center of the dance floor, doing the Typewriter and the Lawn Mower and the Toaster and all the other stupid dances he used to practice when we watched MTV. He would have remembered that daisies were my favorite flower, and he would've made friends with Taylor's boyfriend, Davis, and all the other girls would have been looking at him, wishing he was their date.

chapter *twelve*

From the start, I knew it wasn't going to be easy to get Conrad to go. He wasn't a prom kind of person. But the thing was, I didn't care. I just really wanted him to go with me, to be my date. It had been seven months since the first time we'd kissed. Two months since the last time I'd seen him. One week since the last time he'd called.

Being a person's prom date is definable; it's a real thing. And I had this fantasy of prom in my head, what it would be like. How he would look at me, how when we slow danced, he'd rest his hand on the small of my back. How we'd eat cheese fries at the diner after, and watch the sunrise from the roof of his car. I had it all planned out, how it would go.

When I called him that night, he sounded busy. But I forged ahead anyway. I asked him, "What are you doing the first weekend of April?" My voice trembled when I said the word "April." I was so nervous he'd say no. In fact, deep down I kind of expected him to.

Warily, he asked, "Why?"

"It's my prom."

He sighed. "Belly, I hate dances."

"I know that. But it's my prom, and I really want to go, and I want you to come with me." Why did he have to make everything so hard?

"I'm in college now," he reminded me. "I didn't even want to go to my own prom."

Lightly, I said, "Well, see, that's all the more reason for you to come to mine."

"Can't you just go with your friends?"

I was silent.

"I'm sorry, I just really don't feel like going. Finals are coming up, and it'll be hard for me to drive all the way down for one night."

So he couldn't do this one thing for me, to make me happy. He didn't feel like it. Fine. "That's okay," I told him. "There's plenty of other guys I can go with. No problem."

I could hear his mind working on the other end. "Never mind. I'll take you," he said at last.

"You know what? Don't even worry about it," I said. "Cory Wheeler already asked me. I can tell him I changed my mind."

"Who the hell is Corky Wheeler?"

I smiled. I had him now. Or at least I thought I did. I said, "Cory Wheeler. He plays soccer with Steven. He's a good dancer. He's taller than you."

But then Conrad said, "I guess you'll be able to wear heels, then."

"I guess I will."

I hung up. Was it so much to ask him to be my prom date for one freaking night? And I had lied about Cory Wheeler; he hadn't asked me. But I knew he would, if I let him think I wanted him to.

In bed, under my quilt, I cried a little. I had this perfect prom night in my mind, Conrad in a suit and me in the violet dress my mother bought me two summers ago, the one I had begged for. He had never seen me dressed up before, or wearing heels, for that matter. I really, really wanted him to.

Later he called and I let it go straight to voice mail. On the message, he said, "Hey. I'm sorry about before. Don't go with Cory Wheeler or any other guy. I'll come. You can still wear your heels."

I must have played that message thirty times at least. Even so, I never really listened to what he was actually saying—he didn't want me to go with some other guy, but he didn't want to go with me either.

I wore the violet dress. My mother was pleased, I

could tell. I also wore the pearl necklace Susannah gave me for my sixteenth birthday, and that pleased her too. Taylor and the other girls were all getting their hair done at a fancy salon. I decided to do mine myself. I curled my hair in loose waves and my mother helped with the back. I think the last time she did my hair was in the second grade, when I wore my hair in braids every day. She was good with a curling iron, but then, she was good with most things.

As soon as I heard his car pull into the driveway, I ran to the window. He looked beautiful in his suit. It was black; I'd never seen it before.

I launched myself down the stairs and flung the front door open before he could ring the bell. I couldn't stop smiling and I was about to throw my arms around him when he said, "You look nice."

"Thanks," I said, and my arms fell back at my sides. "So do you."

We must have taken a hundred pictures at the house. Susannah said she wanted photographic proof of Conrad in a suit and me in that dress. My mother kept her on the phone with us. She gave it to Conrad first, and whatever she said to him, he said, "I promise." I wondered what he was promising.

I also wondered if one day, Taylor and I would be like that—on the phone while our kids got ready for the prom. My mother and Susannah's friendship had spanned decades and children and husbands. I wondered if Taylor's and my friendship was made of the same stuff as theirs. Durable, impenetrable stuff. Somehow I doubted it. What they had, it was once-in-a-lifetime.

To me, Susannah said, "Did you do your hair the way we talked about?"

"Yes."

"Did Conrad tell you how pretty you look?"

"Yes," I said, even though he hadn't, not exactly.

"Tonight will be perfect," she promised me.

My mother positioned us on the front steps, on the staircase, standing next to the fireplace. Steven was there with his date, Claire Cho. They laughed the whole time, and when they took their pictures, Steven stood behind her with his arms around her waist and she leaned back into him. It was so easy. In our pictures, Conrad stood stiffly beside me, with one arm around my shoulders.

"Is everything okay?" I whispered.

"Yeah," he said. He smiled at me, but I didn't believe it. Something had changed. I just didn't know what.

I gave him an orchid boutonniere. He forgot to bring my corsage. He'd left it in his little refrigerator back at school, he said. I wasn't sad or mad. I was embarrassed. All this time, I'd made such a big deal about me and Conrad, how we were some kind of couple. But I'd had to beg him to go to the prom with me, and he hadn't even remembered to bring me flowers.

I could tell he felt awful when he realized, right at the moment Steven went to the fridge and came back with a wrist corsage, tiny pink roses to match Claire's dress. He gave her a big bouquet, too.

Claire pulled one of the roses out of her bouquet and handed it to me. "Here," she said, "we'll make you a corsage."

I smiled at her to show I was grateful. "That's okay. I don't want to poke a hole in my dress," I told her. What a crock. She didn't believe me, but she pretended to. She said, "How about we put it in your hair, then? I think it would look really pretty in your hair."

"Sure," I said. Claire Cho was nice. I hoped she and Steven never broke up. I hoped they stayed together forever.

After the thing with the corsage, Conrad tightened up even more. On the way to the car, he grabbed my wrist and said, in a quiet voice, "I'm sorry I forgot your corsage. I should have remembered."

I swallowed hard and smiled without really opening my mouth. "What kind was it?"

"A white orchid," he said. "My mom picked it out."

"Well, for my senior prom, you'll just have to get me two corsages to make up for it," I said. "I'll wear one on each wrist."

I watched him as I said it. We'd still be together in a year, wouldn't we? That was what I was asking.

His face didn't change. He took my arm and said, "Whatever you want, Belly."

In the car, Steven looked at us in the rearview mirror. "Dude, I can't believe I'm going on a double date with you and my little sister." He shook his head and laughed.

Conrad didn't say anything.

I could already feel the night slipping away from me.

The prom was a joint senior and junior prom. That was the way our school did it. In a way it was nice, because you got to go to prom twice. The seniors got to vote on the theme, and this year, the theme was Old Hollywood. It was at the Water Club, and there was a red carpet and "paparazzi."

The prom committee had ordered one of those kits, those prom packages. It cost a ton of money; they'd fundraised all spring. There were all of these old movie posters on the walls, and a big blinking Hollywood sign. The dance floor was supposed to look like a movie set, with lights and a fake camera on a tripod. There was even a director's chair off to the side.

We sat at a table with Taylor and Davis. With her four-and-a-half-inch stilettos, they were the same height.

Conrad hugged Taylor hello, but he didn't make much of an effort to talk to her or to Davis. He was uncomfortable in his suit, just sitting there. When Davis opened up his jacket and showed off his silver flask to Conrad, I cringed. Maybe Conrad *was* too old for all this.

Then I saw Cory Wheeler out on the dance floor, in the center of a circle of people, including my brother and Claire. He was break dancing.

I leaned in close to Conrad and whispered, "That's Cory."

"Who's Cory?" he said.

I couldn't believe he didn't remember. I just couldn't believe it. I stared at him for a second, searching his face, and then I moved away from him. "Nobody," I said.

After we'd been sitting there a few minutes, Taylor grabbed my hand and announced we were going to the bathroom. I was actually relieved.

In the bathroom, she reapplied her lip gloss and whispered to me, "Davis and I are going to his brother's dorm room after the after-prom."

"For what?" I said, rummaging around my little purse for my own lip gloss.

She handed me hers. "For, you know. To be *alone*." Taylor widened her eyes for emphasis.

"Really? Wow," I said slowly. "I didn't know you liked him that much."

"Well, you've been really busy with all your Conrad drama. Which, by the way, he looks hot, but why is he being so lame? Did you guys have a fight?"

"No . . ." I couldn't look her in the eyes, so I just kept applying lip gloss.

"Belly, don't take his shit. This is your prom night. I mean, he's your boyfriend, right?" She fluffed out her hair, posing in the mirror and pouting her lips. "At least make him dance with you."

When we got back to the table, Conrad and Davis were talking about the NCAA tournament, and I relaxed a little. Davis was a UConn fan, and Conrad liked UNC. Mr. Fisher's best friend had been a walk-on for the team, and Conrad and Jeremiah were both huge fans. Conrad could talk about Carolina basketball forever.

A slow song came on then, and Taylor took Davis by the hand and they headed out to the dance floor. I watched them dance, her head on his shoulder, his hands on her hips. Pretty soon, Taylor wouldn't be a virgin anymore. She always said she'd be first.

"Are you thirsty?" Conrad asked me.

"No," I said. "Do you want to dance?"

He hesitated. "Do we have to?"

I tried to smile. "Come on, you're the one who supposedly taught me how to slow dance."

Conrad stood up and offered me his hand. "So let's dance."

I gave him my hand and followed him to the middle of the dance floor. We slow danced, and I was glad the music was loud so he couldn't hear my heart beating.

"I'm glad you came," I said, looking up at him.

"What?" he asked.

Louder, I said, "I said, I'm glad you came."

"Me too." His voice sounded odd; I remember that, the way his voice caught.

Even though he was standing right in front of me, his hands around my waist, mine around his neck, he had never felt so far away.

After, we sat back down at our table. He said, "Do you want to go somewhere?"

"Well, the after-prom doesn't start till midnight," I said, fiddling with my pearl necklace. I wound it around my fingers. I couldn't look at him.

Conrad said, "No, I mean just you and me. Somewhere we can talk."

All of a sudden, I felt dizzy. If Conrad wanted to go somewhere where we could be alone, where we could talk, it meant he wanted to break up with me. I knew it.

"Let's not go anywhere, let's just stay here for a while," I said, and I tried hard not to sound desperate.

"All right," he said.

So we sat there, watching everyone around us dance, their faces shiny, makeup running. I pulled the flower out of my hair and put it in my purse.

When we had been quiet awhile, I said, "Did your mom make you come?" It broke my heart to ask, but I had to know.

"No," he said, but he waited too late to answer.

In the parking lot, it had started to drizzle. My hair, my hair that I had spent the whole afternoon curling, was already falling flat. We were walking to the car when Conrad said, "My head is killing me."

I stopped walking. "Do you want me to go back inside and see if anybody has an aspirin?"

"No, that's okay. You know what, I might head back to school. I have that exam on Monday and everything. Would it be all right if I didn't go to the after-prom? I could still drop you off." He didn't meet my eyes when he spoke.

"I thought you were spending the night."

Conrad fumbled with his car keys and mumbled, "I know, but I'm thinking now that I should get back. . . ." His voice trailed off.

"But I don't want you to leave," I said, and I hated the way I sounded like I was begging.

He jammed his hands inside his pants pockets. "I'm sorry," he said.

We stood there in the parking lot, and I thought, *If we get inside his car, it's all over. He'll drop me off and then he'll drive back to school and he'll never come back. And that'll be it.*

"What happened?" I asked him, and I could feel the panic rising up in my chest. "Did I do something wrong?"

He looked away. "No. It's not you. It has nothing to do with you."

I grabbed his arm, and he flinched. "Will you please just talk to me? Will you tell me what's going on?"

Conrad didn't say anything. He was wishing he was already in his car, driving away. From me. I wanted to hit him.

I said, "Okay, fine, then. If you won't say it, I will."

"If I won't say what?"

"That we're over. That, whatever this is, it's over. I mean, it is, right?" I was crying, and my nose was running, and it was all mixed up in the rain. I wiped my face with the back of my arm.

He hesitated. I saw him hesitate, weigh his words. "Belly—"

"Don't," I said, backing away from him. "Just don't. Don't say anything to me."

"Just wait a minute," he said. "Don't leave it like this."

"You're the one leaving it like this," I said. I started to walk away, as fast as my feet could go in those stupid heels.

"Wait!" he yelled.

I didn't turn around, I walked faster. Then I heard him slam his fist on the hood of his car. I almost stopped.

Maybe I would have if he'd followed me. But he didn't. He got in his car and he left, just like he said he would.

The next morning, Steven came to my room and sat at my desk. He'd just gotten home. He was still wearing his tux. "I'm asleep," I told him, rolling over.

"No, you're not." He paused. "Conrad's not worth it, okay?"

I knew what it cost him to say that to me, and I loved him for it. Steven was Conrad's number one fan; he always had been. When Steven got up and left, I repeated it to myself. *He's not worth it.*

When I came downstairs the next day around lunchtime, my mother said, "Are you all right?"

I sat down at the kitchen table and put my head down. The wood felt cool and smooth against my cheek. I looked up at her and said, "So I guess Steven blabbed."

Carefully, she said, "Not exactly. I did ask him why Conrad didn't stay the night like we planned."

"We broke up," I said. In a way, it was exciting to hear it said out loud, because if we were broken up, that meant that at one point, we had been together. We were real.

My mother sat down across from me. She sighed. "I was afraid this was going to happen."

"What do you mean?"

"I mean, it's more complicated than just you and Conrad. There are more people involved than just the two of you."

I wanted to scream at her, to tell her how insensitive, how cruel she was, and couldn't she see my heart was literally breaking? But when I looked up at her face, I bit back the words and swallowed them down. She was right. There was more to worry about than just my stupid heart. There was Susannah to think of. She was going to be so disappointed. I hated to disappoint her.

"Don't worry about Beck," my mother told me, her voice gentle. "I'll tell her. You want me to fix you something to eat?"

I said yes.

Later, in my room, alone again, I told myself it was better this way. That he'd been wanting to end things all along, so it was better that I said it first. I didn't believe a word of it. If he'd called and asked for me back, if he'd showed up at the house with flowers or a stereo on his shoulders playing our song—did we even have a song? I didn't know, but if he'd made even the tiniest gesture, I'd have taken him back, gladly. But Conrad didn't call.

When I found out Susannah was worse, that she wasn't going to get any better, I called, once. He didn't pick up, and I didn't leave a message. If he had picked up, if he'd called me back, I don't know what I would have said.

And that was it. We were over.

chapter *thirteen*
JEREMIAH

When my mom found out Conrad was taking Belly to prom, she freaked out. She was insanely happy. You'd have thought they were getting married or something. I hadn't seen her happy like that in a long time, and part of me was glad that he could give her that. But mostly I was just jealous. My mom kept calling him at school, reminding him of things like to make sure he rented his tux in time. She said maybe he could borrow mine, and I said I doubted it would fit. She left it at that, which I was relieved about. I ended up going to some girl from Collegiate's prom that night so he couldn't have worn it anyway. The point is, even if he could have, I wouldn't have wanted him to.

She made him promise that he'd be sweet to her, the perfect gentleman. She said, "Make it a night she'll always remember."

When I got home the afternoon after prom, Conrad's car was in the driveway, which was weird. I'd thought he was staying at Laurel's house and then going straight back to school. I stopped by his room, but he was asleep, and pretty soon after, I passed out too.

That night we ordered Chinese food that Mom said she was in the mood for, but when it came, she didn't eat any.

We ate in the TV room, on the couch, something we never did before she got sick. "So?" she asked, looking at Conrad all eagerly. It was the most energetic I'd seen her all day.

He was shoving a spring roll down his throat, like he was in some big hurry. And he'd brought all this laundry home with him, like he expected Mom to do it. "So what?" he asked.

"So you made me wait all day to hear about the prom! I want to know everything!"

"'Oh, that,'" he said. He had this embarrassed look on his face, and I knew he didn't want to talk about it. I was sure he'd done something to screw it up.

"'Oh, that,'" my mom teased. "Come on, Connie, give me some details. How did she look in her dress? Did you dance? I want to hear everything. I'm still waiting on Laurel to email me the pictures."

"It was okay," Conrad said.

"That's it?" I said. I was annoyed with him that night,

with everything about him. He'd gotten to take Belly to her prom and he acted like it was some big chore. If it had been me, I would have done it right.

Conrad ignored me. "She looked really pretty. She wore a purple dress."

My mom nodded, smiling. "I know exactly the one. How'd the corsage look?"

He shifted in his seat. "It looked nice."

"Did you end up getting the kind you pin on or the kind you wear on your wrist?"

"The kind you pin on," he said.

"And did you dance?"

"Yeah, a lot," he said. "We danced, like, every song."

"What was the theme?"

"I don't remember," Conrad said, and when my mother looked disappointed he added, "I think it was A Night on the Continent. It was, like, a tour of Europe. They had a big Eiffel Tower with Christmas tree lights on it, and a London Bridge you could walk across. And a Leaning Tower of Pisa."

I looked over at him. A Night on the Continent was our school's prom theme last year; I know because I was there.

But I guess my mother didn't remember, because she said, "Oh, that sounds so nice. I wish I could've been at Laurel's house to help Belly get ready. I'm gonna call Laure tonight and bug her to send me those pictures.

When do you think you'll get the professional pictures back? I want to get them framed."

"I'm not sure," he said.

"Ask Belly, will you?" She set her plate down on the coffee table and leaned back against the couch cushions. She looked exhausted all of a sudden.

"I will," he said.

"I think I'm going to bed now," she said. "Jere, will you get all this cleaned up?"

"Sure, Mom," I said, helping her to her feet.

She kissed us both on the cheek and went to her bedroom. We'd moved the study upstairs and put her bedroom downstairs so she didn't have to go up and down the stairs.

When she was gone, I said, sarcastically, "So you guys danced all night, huh?"

"Just leave it," Conrad said, leaning his head back against the couch.

"Did you even go to the prom? Or did you lie to Mom about that, too?"

He glared at me. "Yeah, I went."

"Well, somehow I doubt you guys danced all night," I said. I felt like a jerk but I just couldn't let it go.

"Why do you have to be such a dick? What do you care about the prom?"

I shrugged. "I just hope you didn't ruin it for her. What are you even doing here, anyway?"

I expected him to get pissed, in fact I think I hoped he would. But all he said was, "We can't all be Mr. Prom King." He started closing the takeout boxes. "Are you done eating?" he asked.

"Yeah, I'm done," I said.

chapter *fourteen*

When we drove up to campus, there were people milling around outside on the lawn. Girls were laying out in
shorts and bikini tops, and a group of boys were playing
Ultimate Frisbee. We found parking right in front of
Conrad's dorm and then we slipped inside the build-
ing when a girl stepped out with a laundry basket full
of clothes. I felt so incredibly young, and also lost—I'd
never been there before. It was different than I'd pictured
it. Louder. Busier.

Jeremiah knew the way and I had to hurry to keep up.
He took the stairs two at a time and at the third floor, we
stopped. I followed him down a brightly lit hallway. On
the wall by the elevator there was a bulletin board with a
poster that read, LET'S TALK ABOUT SEX, BABY. There were
STD pamphlets and a breast exam how-to, and neon

condoms were stapled around artfully. "Take one," someone had written in highlighter. "Or three."

Conrad's door had his name on it, and underneath it, the name "Eric Trusky."

His roommate was a stocky, muscular guy with reddish brown hair, and he opened the door wearing gym shorts and a T-shirt. "What's up?" he asked us, his eyes falling on me. He reminded me of a wolf.

Instead of feeling flattered by a college guy checking me out, I just felt grossed out. I wanted to hide behind Jeremiah the way I used to hide behind my mother's skirt when I was five and really shy. I had to remind myself I was sixteen, almost seventeen. Too old to be nervous around a guy named Eric Trusky. Even if Conrad did tell me that Eric was always forwarding him freaky porno videos and stayed on his computer pretty much all day. Except for when he watched his soaps from two to four.

Jeremiah cleared his throat. "I'm Conrad's brother, and this is—our friend," he said. "Do you know where he is?"

Eric opened the door and let us in. "Dude, I have no idea. He just took off. Did Ari call you?"

"Who's Ari?" I asked Jeremiah.

"The RA," he said.

"Ari the RA," I repeated, and the corners of Jeremiah's mouth turned up.

"Who are you?" Eric asked me.

"Belly." I watched him, waiting for a glimmer of recognition, something that let me know that Conrad talked about me, had at least mentioned me. But of course there was nothing.

"Belly, huh? That's cute. I'm Eric," he said, leaning against the wall.

"Um, hi," I said.

"So—Conrad didn't say anything to you before he left?" Jeremiah interjected.

"He barely talks, period. He's like an android." Then he grinned at me. "Well, he talks to pretty girls."

I felt sick inside. What pretty girls? Jeremiah exhaled loudly and clasped his hands behind his head. Then he took out his phone and looked at it, as if there might be some answer there.

I sat down on Conrad's bed—navy sheets and navy comforter. It was unmade. Conrad always made his bed at the summer house. Hotel corners and everything.

So this was where he'd been living. This was his life now.

He didn't have a lot of things in his dorm room. No TV, no stereo, no pictures hanging up. Certainly none of me, but none even of Susannah or his dad. Just his computer, his clothes, some shoes, books.

"I was actually about to take off, dudes. Going to my parents' country house. Will you guys just make sure the door is closed when you leave? And when you find C, tell him he owes me twenty bucks for the pizza."

"No worries, man. I'll tell him." I could tell Jeremiah didn't like Eric, the way his lips almost but didn't quite form a smile when he said it. He sat down at Conrad's desk, surveying the room.

Someone knocked on the door and Eric ambled over to open it. It was a girl, wearing a long-sleeved shirt and leggings and sunglasses on the top of her head. "Have you seen my sweater?" she asked him. She peered around him like she was looking for something. Someone.

Did they date, I wondered? That was my first thought. My second thought was, *I'm prettier than her.* I was ashamed of myself for thinking it, but I couldn't help it. The truth was, it didn't matter who was prettier, her or me. He didn't want me anyway.

Jeremiah jumped up. "Are you a friend of Con's? Do you know where he went?"

She eyed us curiously. I could tell she thought Jeremiah was cute, the way she tucked her hair behind her ears and took her sunglasses off. "Um, yeah. Hi. I'm Sophie. Who are you?"

"His brother." Jeremiah walked over and shook her hand. Even though he was stressed out, he took the time to check her out and give her one of his trademark smiles, which she lapped right up.

"Oh, wow. You guys don't even look alike?" Sophie was one of those people who ended her sentences with a question mark. I could already tell that if I knew her, I would hate her.

"Yeah, we get that a lot," Jeremiah said. "Did Con say anything to you, Sophie?"

She liked the way he called her by her name. She said, "I think he said he was going to the beach, to surf or something? He's so crazy."

Jeremiah looked at me. The beach. He was at the summer house.

When Jeremiah called his dad, I sat on the edge of Conrad's bed and pretended not to listen. He told Mr. Fisher that everything was fine, that Conrad was safe in Cousins. He did not mention that I was with him.

He said, "Dad, I'll go get him, it's no big deal."

Mr. Fisher said something on his end, and Jeremiah said, "But Dad—" Then he looked over at me, and mouthed, *Be right back.*

He headed into the hallway and shut the door behind him.

After he was gone, I lay back onto Conrad's bed and stared up at the ceiling. So this was where he slept every night. I'd known him all my life, but in some ways, he was still a mystery to me. A puzzle.

I got out of bed and went over to his desk. Gingerly, I opened the drawer and found a box of pens, some books, paper. Conrad was always careful with his things. I told myself I wasn't *spying.* I was looking for proof. I was Belly Conklin, Girl Detective.

I found it in the second drawer. A robin's egg blue Tiffany box stuffed way in the back. Even as I was opening it I knew it was wrong, but I couldn't help myself. It was a little jewelry box, and there was a necklace inside, a pendant. I pulled it out and let it dangle. At first I thought it was a figure eight, and that maybe he was dating some girl who ice skated—and I decided I hated her, too. And then I took a closer look, and laid it horizontal in the palm of my hand. It wasn't an eight.

It was infinity.

Which was when I knew. It wasn't for some girl who ice skated or for Sophie down the hall. It was for me. He'd bought it for me. Here was my proof. Proof that he really did care.

Conrad was good at math. Well, he was good at everything, but he was really good at math.

A few weeks after we started talking on the phone, when it had become more routine but no less thrilling, I told him all about how much I hated trig and how badly I was doing in it already. Right away I felt guilty for bringing it up—there I was complaining about math when Susannah had cancer. My problems were so petty and juvenile, so *high school* compared to what Conrad was going through.

"Sorry," I'd said.

"For what?"

"For talking about my crappy trig grade when . . ." My voice trailed off. "When your mom's sick."

"Don't apologize. You can say whatever you want to me." He paused. "And Belly, my mom is getting better. She put on five pounds this month."

The hopefulness in his voice, it made me feel so tender toward him I could have cried. I said, "Yeah, I heard that from my mom yesterday. That's really good news."

"So, okay then. So has your teacher taught you SOH-CAH-TOA yet?"

From then on, Conrad started helping me, all over the phone. At first I didn't really pay attention, I just liked listening to his voice, listening to him explain things. But then he'd quiz me, and I hated to disappoint him. So began our tutoring sessions. The way my mother smirked at me when the phone rang at night, I knew she thought we were having some kind of romance, and I didn't correct her. It was easier that way. And it made me feel good, people thinking we were a couple. I'll admit it. I let them think it. I wanted them to. I knew that it wasn't true, not yet, but it felt like it could be. One day. In the meantime, I had my own private math tutor and I really was starting to get the hang of trig. Conrad had a way of making impossible things make sense, and I never loved him more than during those school nights he spent with me on the phone, going over the same problems over and over, until finally, I understood too.

Jeremiah came back into the room, and I closed my fist around the necklace before he could see it.

"So what's up?" I asked him. "Is your dad mad? What did he say?"

"He wanted to go to Cousins himself, but I told him I'd do it. There's no way Conrad would listen to my dad right now. If my dad came, it would only piss him off more." Jeremiah sat down on the bed. "So I guess we're going to Cousins this summer after all."

As soon as he said it, it became real. In my head, I mean. Seeing Conrad wasn't some faraway pretend thing; it was happening. Just like that I forgot all about my plans to save Conrad and I blurted out, "Maybe you should just drop me off on the way."

Jeremiah stared at me. "Are you serious? I can't deal with this by myself. You don't know how bad it's been. Ever since my mom got sick again, Conrad's been in freaking self-destruct mode. He doesn't give a shit about anything." Jeremiah stopped talking and then said, "But I know he still cares what you think about him."

I licked my lips; they felt very dry all of a sudden. "I'm not so sure about that."

"Well, I am. I know my brother. Will you please just come with me?"

When I thought about the last thing I'd said to Conrad, shame took over and it burned me up inside.

You don't say those kinds of things to a person whose mother just died. You just don't. How could I face him? I just couldn't.

Then Jeremiah said, "I'll get you back in time for your boat party, if that's what you're so worried about."

It was such an un-Jeremiah-like thing to say that it took me right out of my shame spiral and I glared at him. "You think I care about a stupid Fourth of July boat party?"

He gave me a look. "You do love fireworks."

"Shut up," I said, and he grinned. "All right," I said. "You win. I'll come."

"All right, then." He stood up. "I'm gonna go take a leak before we go. Oh, and Belly?"

"Yeah?"

Jeremiah smirked at me. "I knew you were gonna give in. You never had a chance."

I threw a pillow at him and he dodged it and did a little victory lap to the door. "Hurry up and pee, you jerk."

When he was gone, I put the necklace on, underneath my tank top. It had left a little infinity indentation in my hand, I'd been holding on to it so hard.

Why did I do it? Why did I put it on? Why didn't I just put it in my pocket, or leave it in the box? I can't even explain it. All I knew was, I just really, really wanted to wear it. It felt like it belonged to me.

chapter *fifteen*

Before we headed down to the car I grabbed Conrad's textbooks and notebooks and his laptop and stuffed as much as I could into the North Face backpack I'd found in his closet. "This way he'll be able to study for those midterms on Monday," I said, handing Jeremiah the laptop.

He winked and said, "I like the way you think, Belly Conklin."

On the way out, we stopped by Ari the RA's room. His door was open and he was sitting at his desk. Jeremiah popped his head in and said, "Hey, Ari. I'm Conrad's brother, Jeremiah. We found Conrad. Thanks for the heads-up, man."

Ari beamed at him. "No problem." Jeremiah made friends wherever he went. Everyone wanted to be Jeremiah Fisher's friend.

Then we were on our way. Headed straight to Cousins, full stop. We drove with the windows down, the radio up.

We didn't talk much, but this time I didn't mind. I think we were both too busy thinking. Me, I was thinking about the last time I headed down this road. Only, it hadn't been with Jeremiah. It had been with Conrad.

chapter *sixteen*

It was, without a doubt, one of the best nights of my life. Right up there with New Year's Eve at Disney World. My parents were still married and I was nine. We watched fireworks rocket right over Cinderella's palace, and Steven didn't even complain.

When he called, I didn't recognize his voice, partly because I wasn't expecting it and partly because I was still half-asleep. He said, "I'm in my car on my way to your house. Can I see you?"

It was twelve thirty in the morning. Boston was five and a half hours away. He had driven all night. He wanted to see me.

I told him to park down the street and I would meet him on the corner, after my mother had gone to bed. He said he'd wait.

I turned the lights off and waited by the window, watching for the taillights. As soon as I saw his car, I wanted to run outside, but I had to wait. I could hear my mother rustling around in her room, and I knew she would read in bed for at least half an hour before she fell asleep. It felt like torture, knowing he was out there waiting for me, not being able to go to him. It was a crazy idea, because it was winter, and it would be freezing cold in Cousins. But when he suggested it, it felt crazy in a good way.

In the dark I put on my scarf and hat that Granna knit me for Christmas. Then I shut my bedroom door and tiptoed down the hallway to my mother's room, pressing my ear against the door. The light was off and I could hear her snoring softly. Steven wasn't even home yet, which was lucky for me, because he's a light sleeper just like our dad.

My mother was finally asleep; the house was still and silent. Our Christmas tree was still up. We kept the lights on all night because it made it still feel like Christmas, like any minute, Santa could show up with gifts. I didn't bother leaving her a note. I would call her in the morning, when she woke up and wondered where I was.

I crept down the stairs, careful on the creaky step in the middle, but once I was out of the house, I flew down the front steps, across the frosty lawn. It crunched along the bottoms of my sneakers. I forgot to put on my coat. I remembered the scarf and hat, but no coat.

His car was on the corner, right where it was supposed to be. The car was dark, no lights, and I opened the passenger side door like I'd done it a million times before.

I poked my head inside, but I didn't go in, not yet. I wanted to look at him first. It was winter, and he was wearing a gray fleece. His cheeks were pink from the cold, his tan had faded, but he still looked the same. "Hey," I said, and then I climbed inside.

"You're not wearing a coat," he said.

"It's not that cold," I said, even though it was, even though I was shivering as I said it.

"Here," he said, shrugging out of his fleece and handing it to me.

I put it on. It was warm, and it didn't smell like cigarettes. It just smelled like him. So Conrad quit smoking after all. The thought made me smile.

He started the engine.

I said, "I can't believe you're really here."

He sounded almost shy when he said, "Me neither." And then he hesitated. "Are you still coming with me?"

I couldn't believe he even had to ask. I would go anywhere. "Yes," I told him. It felt like nothing else existed outside of that word, that moment. There was just us. Everything that had happened that summer, and every summer before it, had all led up to this. To now.

Sitting next to him in the passenger seat felt like an impossible gift. It felt like the best Christmas gift of my life. Because he was smiling at me, and he wasn't somber, or solemn, or sad, or any of the other s-words I had come to associate with Conrad. He was light, he was ebullient, he was all the best parts of himself.

"I think I'm going to be a doctor," he told me, looking at me sideways.

"Really? Wow."

"Medicine is pretty amazing. For a while, I thought I would want to go into the research end of it, but now I think I'd rather be working with actual people."

I hesitated, and then said, "Because of your mom?"

He nodded. "She's getting better, you know. Medicine is making that possible. She's responding really well to her new treatment. Did your mom tell you?"

"Yeah, she did," I said. Even though she had done no such thing. She probably just didn't want to get my hopes up. She probably didn't want to get her own hopes up. My mother was like that. She didn't allow herself to get excited until she knew it was a sure thing. Not me. Already I felt lighter, happier. Susannah was getting better. I was with Conrad. Everything was happening the way it was supposed to.

I leaned over and squeezed his arm. "It's the best news ever," I said, and I meant it.

He smiled at me, and it was written all over his face: hope.

When we got to the house, it was freezing cold. We cranked the heat up and Conrad started a fire. I watched him squat and tear up pieces of paper and poke at the log gently. I bet he'd been gentle with his dog, Boogie. I bet he used to let Boogie sleep in the bed with him. The thought of beds and sleep suddenly made me nervous. But I shouldn't have been, because after he lit the fire, Conrad sat on the La-Z-Boy and not on the couch next to me. The thought suddenly occurred to me: He was nervous too. Conrad, who was never nervous. Never.

"Why are you sitting all the way over there?" I asked him, and I could hear my heart pounding behind my ears. I couldn't believe I'd been brave enough to actually say what I was thinking.

Conrad looked surprised too, and he came over and sat next to me. I inched closer to him. I wanted him to put his arms around me. I wanted to do all the things I'd only seen on TV and heard Taylor talk about. Well, maybe not all, but some.

In a low voice, Conrad said, "I don't want you to be scared."

I whispered, "I'm not," even though I was. Not scared of him, but scared of everything I felt. Sometimes it was too much. What I felt for him was bigger than the world, than anything.

"Good," he breathed, and then he was kissing me.

He kissed me long and slow and even though we'd kissed once before, I never thought it could be like this. He took his time; he ran his hand along the bottom of my hair, the way you do when you walk past hanging wind chimes.

Kissing him, being with him like that . . . it was cool lemonade with a long straw, sweet and measured and pleasurable in a way that felt infinite. The thought crossed my mind that I never wanted him to stop kissing me. *I could do this forever*, I thought.

We kissed on the couch like that for what could have been hours or minutes. All we did that night was kiss. He was careful, the way he touched me, like I was a Christmas ornament he was afraid of breaking.

Once, he whispered, "Are you okay?"

Once, I put my hand up to his chest and I could feel his heart beating as fast as mine. I snuck a peek at him, and for some reason, it delighted me to see his eyes closed. His lashes were longer than mine.

He fell asleep first. I'd heard something about how you weren't supposed to sleep with a fire still burning, so I waited for it to die down. I watched Conrad sleep for a while. He looked like a little boy, the way his hair fell on his forehead and his eyelashes hit his cheek. I didn't remember him ever looking that young. When I was sure he was asleep, I leaned in, I whispered, "Conrad. There's only you. For me, there's only ever been you."

My mother freaked out when I wasn't home that morning. I missed two calls from her because I was asleep. When she called the third time, furious, I said, "Didn't you get my note?"

Then I remembered I hadn't left one.

She practically growled. "No, I did not see any note. Don't you ever leave in the middle of the night without telling me again, Belly."

"Even if I'm just going for a midnight stroll?" I joked. Me making my mother laugh was a sure thing. I would tell a joke and her anger would evaporate away. I started to sing her favorite Patsy Cline song. "I go out walkin', after midnight, out in the moonlight—"

"Not funny. Where are you?" Her voice was tight, clipped.

I hesitated. There was nothing my mother hated worse than a liar. She'd find out anyway. She was like a psychic. "Um. Cousins?"

I heard her take a breath. "With who?"

I looked over at him. He was listening intently. I wished he wasn't. "Conrad," I said, lowering my voice.

Her reaction surprised me. I heard her breathe again, but this time it was a little sigh, like a sigh of relief. "You're with Conrad?"

"Yes."

"How is he?" It was a strange question, what with her in the middle of being mad at me.

I smiled at him and fanned my face like I was relieved. He winked at me. "Great," I said, relaxing.

"Good. Good," she said, but it was like she was talking to herself. "Belly, I want you home tonight. Are we clear?"

"Yes," I said. I was grateful. I thought she'd demand that we leave right away.

"Tell Conrad to drive carefully." She paused. "And Belly?"

"Yes, Laurel?" She always smiled when I called her by her first name.

"Have fun. This will be your last fun day for a long, long time."

I groaned. "Am I grounded?" Being grounded was a novelty; my mother had never grounded me before, but I guess I had never given her a reason to.

"That is a very stupid question."

Now that she wasn't mad anymore, I couldn't resist. "I thought you said there were no stupid questions?"

She hung up the phone. But I knew I had made her smile.

I closed my phone and faced Conrad. "What do we do now?"

"Whatever we want."

"I want to go on the beach."

So that's what we did. We got bundled up and we ran on the beach in rain boots we found in the mud room.

I wore Susannah's, and they were two sizes too big, and I kept slipping in the sand. I fell on my butt twice. I was laughing the whole time, but I could barely hear it because the wind was howling so loud. When we came back inside, I put my freezing hands on his cheeks and instead of pushing them away, he said, "Ahh, feels good."

I laughed and said, "That's because you're coldhearted."

He put my hands in his coat pockets and said in a voice so soft I wondered if I heard him right, "For everyone else, maybe. But not for you." He didn't look at me when he said it, which is how I knew he meant it.

I didn't know what to say, so instead, I got on my tiptoes and kissed him on the cheek. It was cold and smooth against my lips.

Conrad smiled briefly and then started walking away. "Are you cold?" he asked, his back to me.

"Sort of," I said. I was blushing.

"I'll build another fire," he said.

While he worked on the fire, I found an old box of Swiss Miss hot chocolate in the pantry, next to the Twinings teas and my mother's Chock full o'Nuts coffee. Susannah used to make us hot chocolate on rainy nights, when there was a chill in the air. She used milk, but of course there wasn't any, so I used water.

As I sat on the couch and stirred my cup, watching the mini marshmallows disintegrate, I could feel my heart beating, like, a million times a minute. When I was with him, I couldn't seem to catch my breath.

Conrad didn't stop moving around. He was ripping up pieces of paper, he was poking at the embers, he was squatting in front of the fireplace, shifting his weight back and forth.

"Do you want your cocoa?" I asked him.

He looked back at me. "Okay, sure."

He sat next to me on the couch and drank from the *Simpsons* mug. It had always been his favorite. "This tastes—"

"Amazing?"

"Dusty."

We looked at each other and laughed. "For your information, cocoa is my specialty. And you're welcome," I said, taking my first sip. It did taste a little dusty.

He peered at me and tipped my face up. Then he reached out and rubbed my cheek with his thumb like he was wiping away soot. "Do I have cocoa powder on my face?" I asked, suddenly paranoid.

"No," he said. "Just some dirt—oops, I mean, freckles."

I laughed and slapped him on the arm, and then he grabbed my hand and pulled me closer to him. He pushed my hair out of my eyes, and I worried he could hear the way I drew my breath in when he touched me.

It was getting darker and darker outside. Conrad sighed and said, "I'd better get you back."

I looked down at my watch. It was five o'clock. "Yeah . . . I guess we'd better go."

Neither of us moved. He reached out and wound my hair around his fingers like a spool of yarn. "I love how soft your hair is," he said.

"Thanks," I whispered. I'd never thought of my hair as anything special. It was just hair. And it was brown, and brown wasn't as special as blond or black or red. But the way he looked at it . . . at me. Like it held some kind of fascination for him, like he would never get tired of touching it.

We kissed again, but it was different than the night before. There was nothing slow or lazy about it. The way he looked at me—urgent, wanting me, needing me . . . it was like a drug. It was want-want-want. But it was me who was doing the wanting most of all.

When I pulled him closer, when I put my hands underneath his shirt and up his back, he shivered for a second. "Are my hands too cold?" I asked.

"No," he said. Then he let go of me and sat up. His face was sort of red and his hair was sticking up in the back. He said, "I don't want to rush anything."

I sat up too. "But I thought you already—" I didn't know how to finish the sentence. This was so embarrassing. I'd never done this before.

Conrad turned even redder. He said, "Yeah, I mean, I have. But you haven't."

"Oh," I said, looking down at my sock. Then I looked up. "How do you know I haven't?"

Now he looked red as a beet and he stuttered, "I just

thought you hadn't—I mean, I just assumed—"

"You thought I hadn't done anything before, right?"

"Well, yeah. I mean, no."

"You shouldn't make assumptions like that," I said.

"I'm sorry," he said. He hesitated. "So—you have then?"

I just looked at him.

When he opened his mouth to speak, I stopped him. I said, "I haven't. Not even close."

Then I leaned forward and kissed him on the cheek. It felt like a privilege just to be able to do that, to kiss him whenever I wanted. "You're really sweet to me," I whispered, and I felt so glad and grateful to be there, in that moment.

His eyes were dark and serious when he said, "I just— want to always know that you're okay. It's important to me."

"I am okay," I said. "I'm better than okay."

Conrad nodded. "Good," he said. He stood and gave me his hand to help me up. "Let's get you home, then."

I didn't get home that night until after midnight. We stopped and got dinner at a diner off the highway. I ordered pancakes and french fries, and he paid. When I got home, my mother was so mad. But I didn't regret it. I never regretted it, not for one second. How do you regret one of the best nights of your entire life? You don't. You remember every word, every look. Even when it hurts, you still remember.

chapter *seventeen*

We drove through town, by all the old places, the mini golf course, the crab shack, and Jeremiah drove as fast he could, whistling. I wished he would slow down, make the drive last forever. But it wouldn't, of course. We were almost there.

I reached into my bag and pulled out a little pot of lip gloss. I dabbed some gloss on my lips and yanked my fingers through my hair. It was all tangled because we'd had the windows down, and it was a mess. In my peripheral vision, I could feel Jeremiah's eyes on me. He was probably shaking his head and thinking what a dumb girl I was. I wanted to tell him, I know, I am a dumb girl. I'm no better than Taylor. But I couldn't just walk in and face Conrad with ratty hair.

When I saw his car in the driveway, I could feel my

heart constrict. He was in there. Like a shot, Jeremiah was out of the car and bounding toward the house. He took the stairs two at a time, and I trailed after him.

It was strange; the house still smelled the same. For some reason, I hadn't been expecting that. Maybe with Susannah gone, I'd thought it would all feel different. But it didn't. I almost expected to see her floating around in one of her housedresses, waiting for us in the kitchen.

Conrad actually had the nerve to look annoyed when he saw us. He'd just come in from surfing; his hair was wet and he still had his suit on. I felt dazed—even though it had only been two months, it was like seeing a ghost. The ghost of first love past. His eyes flickered on me for about one second before rounding on Jeremiah. "What the hell are you doing here?" he asked him.

"I'm here to pick you up and take you back to school," Jeremiah said, and I could tell he was working hard to sound relaxed, laid-back. "You really messed up, man. Dad's going out of his mind."

Conrad waved him off. "Tell him to go screw himself. I'm staying."

"Con, you missed two classes and you've got midterms on Monday. You can't just bail. They'll kick you out of summer school."

"That's my problem. And what's she doing here?" He didn't look at me when he said it, and it was like he'd stabbed me in the chest.

I started to back away from them, toward the glass sliding doors. It was hard to breathe.

"I brought her with me to help," Jeremiah said. He looked over at me and then took a breath. "Look, we've got all your books and everything. You can study tonight and tomorrow and then we can head back to school."

"Screw it. I don't care," Conrad said, walking over to the sofa. He peeled off the top of his wetsuit. His shoulders were already getting tan. He sat down on the sofa, even though he was still wet.

"What's your problem?" Jeremiah asked him, his voice just barely even.

"Right now, this is my problem. You and her. Here." For the first time since we'd arrived, Conrad looked me in the eyes. "Why do you want to help me? Why are you even here?"

I opened my mouth to speak, but nothing came out. Just like always, he could devastate me with a look, a word.

Patiently, he waited for me to say something, and when I didn't, he did.

"I thought you never wanted to see me again. You hate me, remember?" His tone was sarcastic, belittling.

"I don't hate you," I said, and then I ran away. I pushed the sliding door open and stepped outside to the porch. I closed the door behind me and ran down the stairs, down to the beach.

I just needed to be on the beach. The beach would make me feel better. Nothing, nothing felt better than the way sand felt beneath my feet. It was both solid and shifting, constant and ever-changing. It was summer.

I sat in the sand and I watched the waves run to shore and then spread out thin like white icing on a cookie. It had been a mistake to come here. Nothing I could say or do would erase the past. The way he'd said "her," with such disdain. He didn't even call me by my name.

After a while, I headed back to the house. Jeremiah was in the kitchen by himself. Conrad was nowhere in sight.

"Well, that went well," he said.

"I never should have come."

Jeremiah ignored me. "Ten to one the only thing he has in the fridge is beer," he said. "Any takers?"

He was trying to make me laugh, but I wouldn't. I couldn't. "Only an idiot would take that bet." I bit my lip. I really, really didn't want to cry.

"Don't let him get to you," Jeremiah said. He pulled on my ponytail and wound it around his wrist like a snake.

"I can't help it." The way he'd looked at me—like I meant nothing to him, less than nothing.

"He's an idiot; he doesn't mean anything he says," Jeremiah said. He nudged me. "Are you sorry you came?"

"Yes."

Jeremiah smiled at me crookedly. "Well, I'm not. I'm glad you came. I'm glad I'm not dealing with his BS on my own."

Because he was trying, I tried too. I opened up the fridge like I was one of those women from *The Price Is Right*, the women who wore evening gowns and jeweled heels.

"Ta-da," I said. He was right, the only thing inside were two cases of Icehouse. Susannah would've flipped if she could have seen what had become of her Sub-Zero fridge. "What are we going to do?" I asked him.

He looked out the window, to the beach. "We're probably going to have to stay here tonight. I'll work on him; he'll come. I just need some time." He paused. "So how about this. Why don't you go grab some food for dinner, and I'll stay here and talk to Con."

I knew Jeremiah was trying to get rid of me, and I was glad. I needed to get out of that house, away from Conrad. "Clam rolls for dinner?" I asked him.

Jeremiah nodded and I could tell he was relieved. "Sounds good. Whatever you want." He started to pull out his wallet, but I stopped him.

"It's okay."

He shook his head. "I don't want you to use your money," he said, handing me two creased twenties and his keys. "You already came all this way to help."

"I wanted to."

"Because you're a good person and you wanted to help Con," he said.

"I wanted to help you, too," I told him. "I meant, I still do. You shouldn't have to deal with this on your own."

For one brief moment, he didn't look like himself. He looked like his father. "Who else will?" And then he smiled at me, and he was Jeremiah again. Susannah's boy, sunshine and smiles. Her little angel.

I learned to drive stick on Jeremiah's car. It felt good to be in the driver's seat again. Instead of turning on the AC, I rolled down the windows and let the salty air in. I drove into town slowly, and I parked the car by the old Baptist church.

There were kids running around in bathing suits and shorts, and also parents in khaki, and golden retrievers without leashes. It was probably the first weekend since school let out, for most of them. There was just that feeling in the air. I smiled when I saw a boy trailing after two older girls, probably his sisters. "Wait up," he yelled, his flip flops slapping along the pavement. They just walked faster, not looking back.

My first stop was the general store. I used to spend hours in there, mulling over the penny candy. Each choice seemed vitally important. The boys would dump candy in haphazardly, a scoop of this, a handful of that. But I was careful, ten big Swedish Fish, five malt balls, a medium-size scoop of pear Jelly Bellys. For old times' sake, I filled a bag. I put in Goobers for Jeremiah, a Clark Bar for Conrad, and even though he wasn't here, a Lemonhead for Steven. It was a candy memorial, a tribute to the Cousins of our childhood, when picking penny candy was the biggest and best part of our day.

I was standing in line waiting to pay when I heard someone say, "Belly?"

I turned around. It was Maureen O'Riley, who owned the fancy hat shop in town—Maureen's Millinery. She was older than my parents, in her late fifties, and she was friendly with my mother and Susannah. She took her hats very seriously.

We hugged, and she smelled the same, like Murphy Oil Soap.

"How's your mother? How's Susannah?" she asked me.

"My mother's fine," I told her. I moved up in line, away from Maureen.

She moved up with me. "And Susannah?"

I cleared my throat. "Her cancer came back, and she passed away."

Maureen's tan face wrinkled up in alarm. "I hadn't heard. I'm sorry to hear that. I was very fond of her. When?"

"Beginning of May," I said. It was almost my turn to pay, and then I could leave and this conversation would be over.

Then Maureen clasped my hand, and my first impulse was to snatch it away, even though I'd always liked Maureen. I just didn't want to stand in the general store, talking about Susannah being dead like it was town gossip. We were talking about Susannah here.

She must have sensed it, because she let go. She said, "I wish I'd known. Please send my condolences to the boys and your mother. And Belly, come by the store and see me sometime. We'll get you fitted for a hat. I think it's time you had one, something with a trim."

"I've never worn a hat," I said, fumbling for my wallet.

"It's time," Maureen said again. "Something to set you off. Come by, I'll take care of you. A present."

After, I walked through town slowly, stopping at the bookstore and the surf shop. I walked aimlessly, dipping my hand into the candy bag on occasion. I didn't want to run into anybody else but I was in no hurry to get back to the house. It was obvious Conrad didn't want me around. Was I making things worse? The way he'd looked at me . . . it was harder than I'd thought it was going to be, seeing him again. Being in that house again. A million times harder.

When I got back to the house with the rolls in a greasy paper bag, Jeremiah and Conrad were drinking beer out on the back deck. The sun was setting. It was going to be a beautiful sunset.

I threw the keys and the bag down on the table and

fell onto a lounge chair. "Pass me a beer," I said. It wasn't because I particularly liked beer. I didn't. It was because I wanted to be a part of them, the way having a few beers out back had brought them together in some small way. Just like the old days, all I wanted was to be included.

I expected Conrad to glare at me and tell me no, he would not be passing me any beer. When he didn't, I was surprised to feel disappointed. Jeremiah reached into the cooler and threw me an Icehouse. He winked at me. "Since when does our Belly Button drink?" he said.

"I'm almost seventeen," I reminded him. "Don't you think I'm too old for you to call me that?"

"I know how old you are," Jeremiah said.

Conrad reached into the paper bag and pulled out a sandwich. He bit into it hungrily, and I wondered if he had eaten anything all day.

"You're welcome," I told him. I couldn't help myself. He hadn't looked my way once since I got back. I wanted to make him acknowledge me.

He grunted thanks, and Jeremiah shot me a warning look. Like, *Don't piss him off just when things are good.*

Jeremiah's phone buzzed on the table, and he didn't move to pick it up. Conrad said, "I'm not leaving this house. Tell him that."

My head jerked up. What did that mean, he wasn't leaving? Like, ever? I stared hard at Conrad, but his face was as impassive as ever.

Jeremiah stood up, picked up the phone, and walked back into the house. He closed the sliding door behind him. For the first time, Conrad and I were left to ourselves. The air between us felt heavy, and I wondered if he was sorry for what he'd said earlier. I wondered if I should say something, try and fix things. But what would I say? I didn't know if there was anything I *could* say.

So I didn't try. Instead I let the moment pass and I just sighed and leaned back onto my chair. The sky was pinky gold. I had the feeling that there was nothing more beautiful than this, that this particular sunset matched the beauty of anything in this world, ten times over. I could feel all the tension of the day drifting away from me and out to sea. I wanted to memorize it all in case I didn't get to come back again. You never know the last time you'll see a place. A person.

chapter *eighteen*

We sat around watching TV for a while. Jeremiah didn't make any more moves to talk to Conrad, and no one mentioned school or Mr. Fisher. I wondered if Jeremiah was waiting to be alone with him again.

I forced myself to yawn. To no one in particular, I said, "I'm so tired."

As soon as I said it, I realized I really was. I was so tired. It felt like it had been the longest day ever. Even though all I really did was ride around in a car, I felt completely drained of energy.

"I'm going to sleep," I announced, yawning again, this time for real.

"Good night," Jeremiah said, and Conrad didn't say anything.

As soon as I got to my room, I opened my overnight

bag, and I was horrified when I saw what was inside. There was Taylor's brand-new gingham bikini, her prized platform sandals, an eyelet sundress, the cutoffs that her dad referred to as "denim underwear," a few silky tops, and instead of the big T-shirt I'd been looking forward to wearing to sleep, a pink pajama set with little red hearts. Little shorts and a matching tank top. I wanted to kill her. I'd assumed she was adding to what I'd already packed, not replacing it. The only thing she'd left of mine was the underwear.

The thought of prancing around the house in those pajamas, being seen on the way to brush my teeth in the morning, made me want to hit her. Hard. I knew that Taylor meant well. She thought she was doing me a favor. Giving up her platform sandals for the night was altruistic, for Taylor. But I was still mad.

It was just like the thing with Cory. Taylor did what she wanted to do, and she didn't care what I thought about it. She never cared what I thought about it. It wasn't just her fault though, because I let her.

After I brushed my teeth, I put on Taylor's pajamas and got into bed. I was deliberating over whether or not to read a book before I went to sleep, one of the old paperbacks on my shelf, when someone knocked on my door. I pulled the covers up to my neck and said, "Come in!"

It was Jeremiah. He closed the door behind him and sat at the foot of my bed. "Hey," he whispered.

I loosened the grip on my covers. It was only Jeremiah. "Hey. What's going on? Did you talk to him?"

"Not yet. I'm gonna ease up on him tonight and try again tomorrow. I'm just trying to lay down the ground-work first, plant some seeds." He gave me a conspiratorial look. "You know how he is."

I did. "Okay. That sounds good."

He held his hand out for a high five. "Don't worry. We've got this."

I high-fived him. "We've got this," I repeated. I could hear the doubt in my voice, but Jeremiah just smiled like it was already a done deal.

chapter *nineteen*
JEREMIAH

When Belly got up to go to bed, I knew she wanted me to stay and try to talk to Conrad about school. I knew it because when we were little kids, we used to practice ESP on each other. Belly was convinced I could read her mind and she could read mine. The truth was, I could just read Belly. Whenever she was about to tell a lie, her left eye squinted a little. Whenever she was nervous, she sucked in her cheeks before she spoke. She was an easy read, always had been.

I looked over at Conrad. "Wanna get up early and surf tomorrow?" I asked him.

"Sure," he said.

Tomorrow I would talk to him about school and how important it was to go back. Everything would work out.

We watched some more TV, and when Conrad fell asleep on the couch, I went upstairs to my room. Down the hall, Belly's light was still on. I went over and stood outside her door and knocked softly. I felt like such an idiot standing outside her doorway, knocking. When we were kids, we just ran in and out of each other's rooms without thinking. I wished it was still as simple as that.

"Come in," she said.

I walked in and sat at the edge of her bed. When I realized she was already in her pajamas, I almost turned right back around and left. I had to remind myself that I'd seen her in her pajamas a million times before, and what was the big deal? But she used to always wear a big T-shirt like the rest of us, and now she was wearing some skimpy pink top with little straps. I wondered if it was comfortable to sleep in.

chapter *twenty*

JULY 4

When I woke up the next morning, I didn't get out of bed right away. I just laid there and pretended like it was any other morning at the summer house. My sheets smelled the same; my stuffed bear, Junior Mint, was still sitting on the dresser. It was just like always. Susannah and my mother were taking a walk on the beach, and the boys were eating all the blueberry muffins and leaving me with my mother's Kashi cereal. There would be about an inch of milk left, and no juice, either. It used to infuriate me; now I smiled at the thought.

But it was all make-believe. I knew that. There was no mother, no brother, no Susannah here.

Even though I had gone to bed early the night before, I slept late. It was already almost eleven. I had slept for twelve hours. I hadn't slept that well in weeks.

I got out of bed and went to look out my window. Looking out my bedroom window at the summer house always made me feel better. I wished every window looked out at an ocean, nothing but miles and miles of sand and sea. Down the beach, Jeremiah and Conrad were bobbing on surfboards in black wetsuits. It was such a familiar sight. And just like that, I was hopeful. Maybe Jeremiah was right. Maybe Conrad would come back with us after all.

And then I would go back home, away from him and from everything he reminded me of. I would lay out at the neighborhood pool and I would hang by the snack bar with Taylor, and pretty soon the summer would go by. I would forget how it used to be.

This time really was the last time.

Before I did anything else, I called Taylor. I explained how we were all in Cousins, how we just needed to convince Conrad to go back to school and finish out summer session.

The first thing she said was, "Belly, what do you think you're doing?"

"What do you mean?"

"You know what I mean. This whole situation is messed up. You should be at home where you belong."

I sighed.

"What do you care if Conrad is a college dropout?"

she said. "Let him be a loser if he wants."

Even though I knew no one could hear me, I lowered my voice. "He's going through a lot right now. He needs us."

"He needs his brother. Who, by the way, is hotter than him, hello! Conrad doesn't need you. He cheated on you, remember?"

I was whispering now. "He didn't cheat on me and you know it. We were already broken up. It's not like we were ever even a real couple in the first place." The last part was hard to say.

"Oh, right—he didn't cheat on you, he dumped you right after the prom. What an *amazing* guy."

I ignored her. "Will you please still cover for me if my mom calls?"

She sniffed. "Duh. I happen to be a loyal friend."

"Thank you. Oh, and thank you *so much* for taking all my clothes."

"You're welcome," she said all smug. "And Belly?"

"Yes?"

"Don't lose sight of the mission at hand."

"Well, Jeremiah's been working on him—"

"Not that, dummy. I'm talking about *the mission*. You have to get Conrad to want you back, and then you have to rebuff him. Brutally."

I was glad we were on the phone so she couldn't see me roll my eyes. But the thing was, she had a point. Taylor never got hurt because she was the one who was in charge. She called the shots. Boys wanted her, not the other way around. She was always quoting that line from *Pretty Woman*, the one about being a hooker. "I say who, I say when, I say who."

It wasn't that the idea didn't appeal to me. It was just that it would never work. Getting Conrad to notice me the first time around, however briefly, had been nearly impossible. It wouldn't work a second time.

After Taylor and I hung up, I called my mother. I told her that I was staying at Taylor's house again that night, that she was still too upset for me to leave. My mother agreed. "You're a good friend," she said. There was relief in her voice when she asked me to tell Taylor's parents hello.

She didn't even question the lie. I could hear it over the phone: All she wanted was to be left alone with her grief.

After, I took a shower and put on the clothes Taylor picked for me. A white camisole with flowers embroidered across the top and her famous cutoffs.

I went downstairs with my hair still wet, tugging on my shorts. The boys were back inside, sitting at the kitchen table and eating dirt bombs, the big sugary cinnamon muffins that Susannah used to get up early to buy.

"Look what I got," Jeremiah said. He pushed the white paper bag toward me.

I grabbed the bag and stuffed half a dirt bomb inside

my mouth. It was still warm. "Yum," I said, my mouth full. "So . . . what's up?"

Jeremiah looked at Conrad hopefully. "Con?"

"You guys should head out soon, if you want to miss the Fourth of July traffic," Conrad said, and it killed me to see the look on Jeremiah's face.

"We're not leaving without you," Jeremiah told him.

Conrad exhaled. "Look, Jere, I appreciate you coming here. But as you can see, I'm fine. I've got everything under control."

"Like hell you do. Con, if you're not back on Monday for your exams, you're out. The only reason you're even taking summer school is those incompletes from last semester. If you don't go back, then what?"

"Don't worry about it. I'll figure things out."

"You keep saying that, but dude, you haven't figured out shit. All you've done so far is run away."

The way Conrad glared at him, I knew that Jeremiah had said the right thing. Conrad's old value system was still there, buried underneath the anger. The old Conrad would never give up.

It was my turn to say something. I took a breath and said, "So, how are you going to become a doctor without a college degree, Conrad?"

He did a double take, and then he stared at me. I stared right back. Yeah, I said it. I would say whatever I had to, even if it hurt him.

It was something I'd learned from watching Conrad in pretty much every game we'd ever played. At the first sign of weakness, you attack full force. You strike and you use every weapon in your arsenal, and you don't let up. No mercy.

"I never said I was going to be a doctor," he snapped. "You don't know what you're talking about."

"Then tell us," I said, and my heart was beating so fast.

No one spoke. For a minute, I thought he might really let us in.

And then finally, Conrad stood up. "There's nothing to tell. I'm gonna head back out there. Thanks for the dirt bombs, Jere." To me, he said, "You have sugar all over your face." And just like that, he was up and sliding the porch door open.

When he was gone, Jeremiah shouted, "Shit!"

I said, "I thought you were gonna work on him!" It came out sounding more accusing than I meant it.

"You can't push Conrad too hard, he just shuts down," Jeremiah said, crumbling up the paper bag.

"He's already shut down."

I looked over at Jeremiah and he looked so defeated. I felt like bad for snapping at him. So I reached out and touched his arm, and said, "Don't worry. We still have time. It's only Saturday, right?"

"Right," he said, but he didn't say it like he meant it.

Neither of us said anything more. Like always, it was Conrad who dictated the mood of the house, how everyone else felt. Nothing would feel right again until things were right with Conrad.

chapter *twenty-one*

The first time it hit me that day was when I was in the bathroom, washing the sugar off my face. There was no towel hanging up, so I opened the linen closet, and on the row below the beach towels, there was Susannah's big floppy hat. The one she wore every time she sat on the beach. She was careful with her skin. *Was.*

Not thinking about Susannah, consciously not thinking about her, made it easier. Because then she wasn't really *gone.* She was just off someplace else. That was what I'd been doing since she died. Not thinking about her. It was easier to do at home. But here, at the summer house, she was everywhere.

I picked her hat up, held it for a second, and then put it back on the shelf. I closed the door, and my chest hurt so bad I couldn't breathe. It was too hard. Being there, in this house, was too hard.

I ran up the stairs as fast as I could. I took off Conrad's necklace and I changed out of my clothes and into Taylor's bikini. I didn't care how stupid I looked in it. I just wanted to be in the water. I wanted to be where I didn't have to think about anything, where nothing else existed. I would swim, and float, and breathe in and out, and just be.

My old Ralph Lauren teddy bear towel was in the linen closet just like always. I put it around my shoulders like a blanket and headed outside. Jeremiah was eating an egg sandwich and swigging from a carton of milk. "Hey," he said.

"Hey. I'm going to swim." I didn't ask where Conrad was, and I didn't invite Jeremiah to join me. I needed a moment just by myself.

I pushed the sliding door open and closed it without waiting for him to answer me. I threw my towel onto a chair and swan-dived in. I didn't come up for air right away. I stayed down under; I held my breath until the very last second.

When I came up, I felt like I could breathe again, like my muscles were relaxing. I swam back and forth, back and forth. Here, nothing else existed. Here, I didn't have to think. Each time I went under, I held my breath for as long as I could.

Under water, I heard Jeremiah call my name. Reluctantly I came up to the surface, and he was crouching by the side of the pool. "I'm gonna go out for a while. Maybe I'll pick up a pizza at Nello's," he said, standing up.

I pushed my hair out of my eyes. "But you just ate a sandwich. And you had all those dirt bombs."

"I'm a growing boy. And that was an hour and a half ago."

An hour and a half ago? Had I been swimming for an hour and a half? It felt like minutes. "Oh," I said. I examined my fingers. They were totally pruned.

"Carry on," Jeremiah said, saluting me.

Kicking off the side of the pool, I said, "See ya." Then I swam as quick as I could to the other side and flip-turned, just in case he was still watching. He'd always admired my flip turns.

I stayed in the pool for another hour. When I came up for air after my last lap, I saw that Conrad was sitting in the chair where I'd left my towel. He held it out to me silently.

I climbed out of the pool. Suddenly I was shivering. I took the towel from him and wrapped it around my body. He did not look at me. "Do you still pretend you're at the Olympics?" he asked me.

I started, and then I shook my head and sat down next to him. "No," I said, and the word hung in the air. I hugged my knees to my chest. "Not anymore."

"When you swim," he started to say. I thought he wasn't going to continue, but then he said, "You wouldn't notice if the house was on fire. You're so into what you're doing, it's like you're someplace else."

He said it with grudging respect. Like he'd been watching me for a long time, like he'd been watching me for years. Which I guess he had.

I opened my mouth to respond, but he was already standing up, going back into the house. As he closed the sliding door, I called out, "That's why I like it."

chapter *twenty-two*

I was back in my room, about to change out of my bikini when my phone rang. It was Steven's ringtone, a Taylor Swift song he pretended to hate but secretly loved. For a second, I thought about not answering. But if I didn't pick up, he'd only call back until I did. He was annoying that way.

"Hello?" I said it like a question, like I didn't already know it was Steven.

"Hey," he said. "I don't know where you are, but I know you're not with Taylor."

"How do you know that?" I whispered.

"I just ran into her at the mall. She's worse than you at lying. Where the hell are you?"

I bit my upper lip and I said, "At the summer house. In Cousins."

"What?" he sort of yelled. "Why?"

"It's kind of a long story. Jeremiah needed my help with Conrad."

"So he called *you?*" My brother's voice was incredulous and also the tiniest bit jealous.

"Yeah." He was dying to ask me more, but I was banking on the fact that his pride wouldn't let him. Steven hated being left out. He was silent for a moment, and in those seconds, I knew he was wondering about all the summer house stuff we were doing without him.

At last he said, "Mom's gonna be so pissed."

"What do you care?"

"I don't care, but Mom will."

"Steven, chill out. I'll be home soon. We just have to do one last thing."

"What last thing?" It killed him that I knew something he didn't, that for once, he was the odd man out. I thought I'd take more pleasure in it, but I felt oddly sorry for him.

So instead of gloating the way I normally would, I said, "Conrad took off from summer school and we have to get him back in time for midterms on Monday."

That would be the last thing I would do for him. Get him to school. And then he'd be free, and so would I.

After Steven and I got off the phone, I heard a car pull up in front of the house. I looked out the window and there was a red Honda, a car I didn't recognize. We almost never had visitors at the summer house.

I dragged a comb through my hair and hurried down the stairs with my towel wrapped around me. I stopped when I saw Conrad open the door, and a woman walked in. She was petite, with bleached blond hair that was in a messy bun, and she wore black pants and a silk coral blouse. Her fingernails were painted to match. She had a big folder in her hand and a set of keys.

"Well, hello there," she said. She was surprised to see him, as if she was the one who was supposed to be there and he wasn't.

"Hello," Conrad said. "Can I help you?"

"You must be Conrad," she said. "We spoke on the phone. I'm Sandy Donatti, your dad's real estate agent."

Conrad said nothing.

She wagged her finger at him playfully. "You told me your dad changed his mind about the sale."

When Conrad still said nothing, she looked around and saw me standing at the bottom of the stairs. She frowned and said, "I'm just here to check on the house, make sure everything's coming along and getting packed up."

"Yeah, I sent the movers away," Conrad said casually.

"I really wish you hadn't done that," she said, her lips tight. When Conrad shrugged, she added, "I was told the house would be empty."

"You were given erroneous information. I'll be here for

the rest of the summer." He gestured at me. "That's Belly."

"Belly?" she repeated.

"Yup. She's my girlfriend."

I think I choked out loud.

Crossing his arms and leaning against the wall, he continued. "And you and my dad met how?"

Sandy Donatti flushed. "We met when he decided to put the house up for sale," she snapped.

"Well, the thing is, Sandy, it's not his house to sell. It's my mother's house, actually. Did my dad tell you that?"

"Yes."

"Then I guess he also told you she's dead."

Sandy hesitated. Her anger seemed to evaporate at the mention of dead mothers. She was so uncomfortable, she was shifting toward the door. "Yes, he did tell me that. I'm very sorry for your loss."

Conrad said, "Thank you, Sandy. That means a lot, coming from you."

Her eyes darted around the room one last time. "Well, I'm going to talk things over with your dad and then I'll be back."

"You do that. Make sure you let him know the house is off the market."

She pursed her lips and then opened her mouth to speak, but thought better of it. Conrad opened the door for her, and then she was gone.

I let out a big breath. A million thoughts were running through my head—I'm ashamed to say that *girl-friend* was pretty near the top of the list. Conrad didn't look at me when he said, "Don't tell Jeremiah about the house."

"Why not?" I asked. My mind was still lingering on the word "girlfriend."

He took so long to answer me that I was already walking back upstairs when he said, "I'll tell him about it. I just don't want him to know yet. About our dad."

I stopped walking. Without thinking I said, "What do you mean?"

"You know what I mean." Conrad looked at me, his eyes steady.

I suppose I did know. He wanted to protect Jeremiah from the fact that his dad was an asshole. But it wasn't like Jeremiah didn't already know who his dad was. It wasn't like Jeremiah was some dumb kid without a clue. He had a right to know if the house was for sale.

I guessed Conrad read all of this on my face, because he said in that mocking, careless way of his, "So can you do that for me, Belly? Can you keep a secret from your BFF Jeremiah? I know you two don't keep secrets from each other, but can you handle it just this once?"

When I glared at him, all ready to tell him what he could do with his secret, he said, "Please?" and his voice was pleading.

So I said, "All right. For now."

"Thank you," he said, and he brushed past me and headed upstairs. His bedroom door closed, and the air conditioning kicked on.

I stayed put.

It took a minute for everything to sink in. Conrad didn't just run away to surf. He didn't run away for the sake of running away. He came to save the house.

chapter *twenty-three*

Later that afternoon Jeremiah and Conrad went surfing again. I thought maybe Conrad wanted to tell him about the house, just the two of them. And maybe Jeremiah wanted to try and talk to Conrad about school again, just the two of them. That was fine by me. I was content just watching.

I watched them from the porch. I sat in a deck chair with my towel wrapped tight around me. There was something so comforting and right about coming out of the pool wet and your mom putting a towel around your shoulders, like a cape. Even without a mother there to do it for you, it was good, cozy. Achingly familiar in a way that made me wish I was still eight. Eight was before death or divorce or heartbreak. Eight was just eight. Hot dogs and peanut butter, mosquito bites and splinters, bikes and boogie boards. Tangled hair, sunburned shoulders, Judy Blume, in bed by nine thirty.

I sat there thinking those melancholy kinds of thoughts for a long while. Someone was barbecuing; I could smell charcoal burning. I wondered if it was the Rubensteins, or maybe it was the Tolers. I wondered if they were grilling burgers, or steak. I realized I was hungry.

I wandered into the kitchen but I couldn't find anything to eat. Just Conrad's beer. Taylor told me once that beer was just like bread, all carbohydrates. I figured that even though I hated the taste of it, I might as well drink it if it'd fill me up.

So I took one and walked back outside with it. I sat back down on my deck chair and popped the top off the can. It snapped very satisfyingly. It was strange to be in this house alone. Not a bad feeling, just a different one. I'd been coming to this house my whole life and I could count on one hand the number of times I'd been alone in it. I felt older now. Which I suppose I was, but I guess I didn't remember feeling old last summer.

I took a long sip of beer and I was glad Jeremiah and Conrad weren't there to see me, because I made a terrible face and I knew they'd give me crap for it.

I was taking another sip when I heard someone clear his throat. I looked up and I nearly choked. It was Mr. Fisher.

"Hello, Belly," he said. He was wearing a suit, like he'd

come straight from work, which he probably had, even though it was a Saturday. And somehow his suit wasn't even rumpled, even after a long drive.

"Hi, Mr. Fisher," I said, and my voice came out all nervous and shaky.

My first thought was, *We should have just forced Conrad into the car and made him go back to school and take his stupid tests.* Giving him time was a huge mistake. I could see that now. I should have pushed Jeremiah into pushing Conrad.

Mr. Fisher raised an eyebrow at my beer and I realized I was still holding it, my fingers laced around it so tight they were numb. I set the beer on the ground, and my hair fell in my face, for which I was glad. It was a moment to hide, to figure out what to say next.

I did what I always did—I deferred to the boys. "Um, so, Conrad and Jeremiah aren't here right now." My mind was racing. They would be back any minute.

Mr. Fisher didn't say anything, he just nodded and rubbed the back of his neck. Then he walked up the porch steps and sat in the chair next to mine. He picked up my beer and took a long drink. "How's Conrad?" he asked, setting the beer on his armrest.

"He's good," I said right away. And then I felt foolish, because he wasn't good at all. His mother had just died. He'd run away from school. How could he be good? How could any of us? But I guess, in a sense, he was good, because he had purpose again. He had a reason. To live.

He had a goal; he had an enemy. Those were good incentives. Even if the enemy was his father.

"I don't know what that kid is thinking," Mr. Fisher said, shaking his head.

What could I say to that? I never knew what Conrad was thinking. I was sure not many people did. Even still, I felt defensive of him. Protective.

Mr. Fisher and I sat in silence. Not companionable, easy silence, but stiff and awful. He never had anything to say to me, and I never knew what to say to him. Finally he cleared his throat and said, "How's school?"

"It's over," I said, chewing on my bottom lip and feeling twelve. "Just finished. I'll be a senior this fall."

"Do you know where you want to go to college?"

"Not really." The wrong answer, I knew, because college was one thing Mr. Fisher was interested in talking about. The right kind of college, I mean.

And then we were silent again.

This was also familiar. That feeling of dread, of impending doom. The feeling that I was In Trouble. That we all were.

chapter *twenty-four*

Milk shakes. Milk shakes were Mr. Fisher's thing. When Mr. Fisher came to the summer house, there were milk shakes all the time. He'd buy a Neapolitan carton of ice cream. Steven and Conrad were chocolate, Jeremiah was strawberry, and I liked a vanilla-chocolate mix, like those Frosties at Wendy's. But thick-thick. Mr. Fisher's milk shakes were better than Wendy's. He had a fancy blender he liked to use, that none of us kids were supposed to mess with. Not that he said so, exactly, but we knew not to. And we never did. Until Jeremiah had the idea for Kool-Aid Slurpees.

There were no 7-Elevens in Cousins, and even though we had milk shakes, we sometimes yearned for Slurpees. When it was especially hot outside, one of us would say, "Man, I want a Slurpee," and then all of us would be thinking about it all day. So when Jeremiah had this idea for Kool-Aid Slurpees, it was, like, kismet. He was nine and I was eight, and at the time it sounded like the greatest idea in the world, ever.

We eyed the blender, way up high on the top shelf. We knew we'd have to use it—in fact we *longed* to use it. But there was that unspoken rule.

No one was home but the two of us. No one would have to know.

"What flavor do you want?" he asked me at last.

So it was decided. This was happening. I felt fear and also exhilaration that we were doing this forbidden thing. I rarely broke rules, but this seemed a good one to break.

"Black Cherry," I said.

Jeremiah looked in the cabinet, but there was none. He asked, "What's your second-best flavor?"

"Grape."

Jeremiah said that grape Kool-Aid Slurpee sounded good to him, too. The more he said the words "Kool-Aid Slurpee," the more I liked the sound of it.

Jeremiah got a stool and took the blender down from the top shelf. He poured the whole packet of grape into the blender and added two big plastic cups of sugar. He let me stir. Then he emptied half the ice dispenser into the blender, until it was full to the brim, and he snapped on the top the way we'd seen Mr. Fisher do it a million times.

"Pulse? Frappe?" he asked me.

I shrugged. I never paid close enough attention when Mr. Fisher used it. "Probably frappe," I said, because I liked the sound of the word "frappe."

So Jeremiah pushed frappe, and the blender started to chop and whir. But only the bottom part was getting mixed, so Jeremiah pushed liquefy. It kept at it for a minute, but then the blender started to smell like burning rubber, and I worried it was working too hard with all that ice.

"We've got to stir it up more," I said. "Help it along."

I got the big wooden spoon and took the top off the blender and stirred it all up. "See?" I said.

I put the top back on, but I guess I didn't do it tight enough, because when Jeremiah pushed frappe, our grape Kool-Aid Slurpee went everywhere. All over us. All over the new white counters, all over the floor, all over Mr. Fisher's brown leather briefcase.

We stared at each other in horror.

"Quick, get paper towels!" Jeremiah yelled, unplugging the blender. I dove for the briefcase, mopping it up with the bottom of my T-shirt. The leather was already staining, and it was sticky.

"Oh, man," Jeremiah whispered. "He loves that briefcase."

And he did. It had his initials engraved on the brass clasp. He truly loved it, maybe even more than his blender.

I felt terrible. Tears pricked my eyelids. It was all my fault. "I'm sorry," I said.

Jeremiah was on the floor, on his hands and knees wiping. He looked up at me, grape Kool-Aid dripping down his forehead. "It's not your fault."

"Yeah, it is," I said, rubbing at the leather. My T-shirt was starting to turn brown from rubbing at the briefcase so hard.

"Well, yeah, it kinda is," Jeremiah agreed. Then he reached out and touched his finger to my cheek and licked off some of the sugar. "Tastes good, though."

We were giggling and sliding our feet along the floor with paper towels when everyone came back home. They walked in with long paper bags, the kind the lobsters come in, and Steven and Conrad had ice-cream cones.

Mr. Fisher said, "What the hell?"

Jeremiah scrambled up. "We were just—"

I handed the briefcase over to Mr. Fisher, my hand shaking. "I'm sorry," I whispered. "It was an accident."

He took it from me and looked at it, at the smeared leather. "Why were you using my blender?" Mr. Fisher demanded, but he was asking Jeremiah. His neck was bright red. "You know you're not to use my blender."

Jeremiah nodded. "I'm sorry," he said.

"It was my fault," I said in a small voice.

"Oh, Belly," my mother said, shaking her head at me. She knelt on the ground and picked up the soaked paper towels. Susannah had gone to get the mop.

Mr. Fisher exhaled loudly. "Why don't you ever listen when I tell you something? For God's sake. Did I or did I not tell you to never use this blender?"

Jeremiah bit his lip, and from the way his chin was quivering, I could tell he was really close to crying.

"Answer me when I'm talking to you."

Susannah came back in then with her mop and bucket. "Adam, it was an accident. Let it go." She put her arms around Jeremiah.

"Suze, if you baby him, he'll never learn. He'll just stay a little baby," Mr. Fisher said. "Jere, did I or did I not tell you kids never to use the blender?"

Jeremiah's eyes filled up and he blinked quickly, but a few tears escaped. And then a few more. It was awful. I felt so embarrassed for Jeremiah and also I felt guilty that it was me who had brought all this upon him. But I also felt relieved that it wasn't me who was the one getting in trouble, crying in front of everyone.

And then Conrad said, "But Dad, you never did." He had chocolate ice cream on his cheek.

Mr. Fisher turned and looked at him. "What?"

"You never said it. We knew we weren't supposed to, but you never technically said it." Conrad looked scared, but his voice was matter-of-fact.

Mr. Fisher shook his head and looked back at Jeremiah. "Go get cleaned up," he said roughly. He was embarrassed, I could tell.

Susannah glared at him and swept Jeremiah into the bathroom. My mother was wiping down the counters, her shoulders straight and stiff. "Steven, take your sister to the bathroom," she said. Her voice left no room for argument, and Steven grabbed my arm and took me upstairs.

"Do you think I'm in trouble?" I asked Steven.

He wiped my cheeks roughly with a wet piece of toilet paper. "Yes. But not as much trouble as Mr. Fisher. Mom's gonna rip him a new one."

"What does that mean?"

Steven shrugged. "Just something I heard. It means he's the one in trouble."

After my face was clean, Steven and I crept back into the hallway. My mother and Mr. Fisher were arguing. We looked at each other, our eyes huge when we heard our mother snap, "You can be such an ass-hat, Adam."

I opened my mouth, about to exclaim, when Steven clapped his hand over my mouth and dragged me to the boys' room. He shut the door behind us. His eyes were glittery from all the excitement. Our mother had cussed at Mr. Fisher.

I said, "Mom called Mr. Fisher an ass-hat." I didn't even know what an ass-hat was, but it sure sounded funny. I pictured a hat that looked like a butt sitting on top of Mr. Fisher's big head. And then I giggled.

It was all very exciting and terrible. None of us had ever really gotten in trouble at the summer house. Not big trouble anyway. It was pretty much a big trouble-free zone.

The mothers were relaxed at the summer house. Where at home, Steven would Get It if he talked back, here, my mother didn't seem to mind as much. Probably because at the Cousins house, us kids weren't the center of the world. My mother was busy doing other things, like potting plants and going to art galleries with Susannah and sketching and reading books. She was too busy to get angry or bothered. We did not have her full attention.

This was both a good and bad thing. Good, because we got away with stuff. If we played out on the beach past bedtime, if we had double dessert, no one really cared. Bad, because I had the vague sense that Steven and I weren't as important here, that there were other things that occupied my mother's mind—memories we had no part of, a life before we existed. And also, the secret life inside herself, where Steven and I didn't exist. It was like when she went on her trips without us—I knew that she did not miss us or think about us very much.

I hated that thought, but it was the truth. The mothers had a whole life separate from us. I guess us kids did too.

chapter *twenty-five*

When Jeremiah and Conrad walked up the beach with their boards under their arms, I had this crazy thought that I should try to warn them somehow. Whistle or something. But I didn't know how to whistle, and it was too late anyway.

They put the boards under the house, and then they walked up the steps and saw us sitting there. Conrad's whole body tightened up, and I saw Jeremiah mutter *"shit"* under his breath. Then Jeremiah said, "Hey, Dad." Conrad brushed right past us and into the house.

Mr. Fisher followed him in, and Jeremiah and I looked at each other for a moment. He leaned close to me and said, "How about you pull the car around while I get our stuff, and then we make a run for it?"

I giggled, and then I clapped my hand over my mouth.

I doubted Mr. Fisher would appreciate me giggling when all this serious stuff was going on. I stood up and pulled my towel closer around me, under my armpits. Then we went inside too.

Conrad and Mr. Fisher were in the kitchen. Conrad was opening up a beer, not even looking at his dad. "What the hell are you kids playing at here?" Mr. Fisher said. His voice sounded really loud and unnatural in the house. He was looking around the kitchen, the living room.

Jeremiah began, "Dad—"

Mr. Fisher looked right at Jeremiah and said, "Sandy Donatti called me this morning and told me what happened. You were supposed to get Conrad back to school, not stay and—and party and interfere with the sale."

Jeremiah blinked. "Who's Sandy Donatti?"

"She's our real estate agent," Conrad said.

I realized my mouth was open, and I snapped it shut. I wrapped my arms around myself tight, trying to turn invisible. Maybe it wasn't too late for me and Jeremiah to make a run for it. Maybe that way he'd never find out that I'd known about the house too. Would it make a difference that I'd only known about it since this afternoon? I doubted it.

Jeremiah looked over at Conrad, and then back at his dad. "I didn't know we had a real estate agent. You never told me you were selling the house."

"I told you it was a possibility."

"You never told me you were actually doing it."

Conrad broke in, speaking only to Jeremiah. "It doesn't matter. He's not selling the house." He drank his beer calmly, and we all waited to hear what he'd say next. "It's not his to sell."

"Yes, it is," Mr. Fisher said, breathing heavily. "I'm not doing this for me. The money will be for you boys."

"You think I care about the money?" Conrad finally looked at him, his eyes cold. His voice was toneless. "I'm not like you. I could give a shit about the money. I care about the house. Mom's house."

"Conrad—"

"You have no right to be here. You should leave."

Mr. Fisher swallowed and his Adam's apple bobbed up and down. "No, I won't leave."

"Tell *Sandy* not to bother coming back." Conrad said the word "Sandy" like it was an insult. Which I guess it was meant to be.

"I'm your father," Mr. Fisher said hoarsely. "And your mother left it to me to decide. This is what she would have wanted."

Conrad's smooth, hard shell cracked, and his voice was shaking when he said, "Don't talk about what she would have wanted."

"She was my wife, goddamn it. I lost her too."

That might have been true, but it was the exact wrong thing to say to Conrad at that moment. It set him off.

He punched the wall closest to him, and I flinched. I was shocked he didn't leave a hole.

He said, "You didn't lose her. You left her. You don't know the first thing about what she would have wanted. You were never there. You were a shitty dad and an even shittier husband. So don't bother trying to do the right thing now. You just fuck it all up."

Jeremiah said, "Con, shut up. Just shut up."

Conrad swung around and shouted, "You're still defending him? That's exactly why we didn't tell you!"

"We?" Jeremiah repeated. He looked at me then, and the stricken look on his face cut right through me.

I started to speak, to try to explain, but I only got as far as saying, "I just found out today, I swear," when Mr. Fisher interrupted me.

He said, "You are not the only one hurting, Conrad. You don't get to talk to me that way."

"I think I do."

The room was deadly quiet and Mr. Fisher looked like he might hit Conrad, he was so mad. They stared at each other, and I knew Conrad wouldn't be the one to back down.

It was Mr. Fisher who looked away. "The movers are coming back, Conrad. This is happening. You throwing a tantrum can't stop it."

He left soon after. He said he'd be back in the morning, and the words were ominous. He said that he was staying at the inn in town. It was clear that he couldn't wait to get out of that house.

The three of us stood around in the kitchen after he was gone, none of us saying anything. Least of all me. I wasn't even supposed to be there. For once, I wished I was at home with my mother and Steven and Taylor, away from all of this.

Jeremiah was the first to speak. "I can't believe he's really selling the house," he said, almost to himself.

"Believe it," Conrad said harshly.

"Why didn't you tell me about it?" Jeremiah demanded.

Conrad glanced at me before saying, "I didn't think you needed to know."

Jeremiah's eyes narrowed. "What the hell, Conrad? It's my house too."

"Jere, I only just found out myself." Conrad propped himself up on the kitchen counter, his head down. "I was at home picking up some clothes. That real estate agent, Sandy, called and left a message on the machine, saying movers were coming to get the stuff they packed. I went back to school and got my stuff and I came straight here."

Conrad had dropped school and everything else to come to the summer house, and here we'd just thought he was a screwup in need of saving. When in actuality, he was the one doing the saving.

I felt guilty for not giving him the benefit of the

doubt, and I knew Jeremiah did too. We exchanged a quick look and I knew we were thinking exactly the same thing. Then I guess he remembered he was pissed at me, too, and he looked away.

"So that's it, then?" Jeremiah said.

Conrad didn't answer him right away. Then he looked up and said, "Yeah, I guess it is."

"Well, great job taking care of all this, Con."

"I've been handling this on my own," Conrad snapped. "It's not like I had any help from you."

"Well, maybe if you'd told me about it—"

Conrad cut him off. "You'd have done what?"

"I would have talked to Dad."

"Yeah, exactly." Conrad could not have sounded more disdainful.

"What the hell does that mean?"

"It means that you're so busy being up his ass, you can't see him for who he is."

Jeremiah didn't say anything right away, and I was really afraid of where this was heading. Conrad was looking for a fight and the last thing we needed was for the two of them to start wrestling on the kitchen floor, breaking things and each other. This time, my mother wasn't here to stop them. There was just me, and that was hardly anything.

And then Jeremiah said, "He's our father." His voice was measured, even, and I let out a tiny breath of relief.

There wouldn't be any fight, because Jeremiah wouldn't let it happen. I admired him for that.

But Conrad just shook his head in disgust. "He's a dirtbag."

"Don't call him that."

"What kind of guy cheats on his wife and then leaves her when she has cancer? What kind of man does that? I can't even stand to look at him. He makes me sick, playing the martyr now, the grieving widower. But where was he when Mom needed him, huh, Jere?"

"I don't know, Con. Where were you?"

The room went silent, and it felt to me like the air was almost crackling. The way Conrad flinched, the way Jeremiah sucked in his breath right after he said it. He wanted to take it back, I could tell, and he was about to, when Conrad said, conversationally, "That's a low blow."

"I'm sorry," Jeremiah said.

Conrad shrugged, brushing him off like it didn't matter either way.

And then Jeremiah said, "Why can't you just let it go? Why do you have to hold on to all the shitty stuff that's ever happened to you?"

"Because I live in reality, unlike you. You'd rather live in a fantasy world than see people for who they really are." He said it in a way that made me wonder who he was really talking about.

Jeremiah bristled. He looked at me and then back at

Conrad and said, "You're just jealous. Admit it."

"Jealous?"

"You're jealous that Dad and I have an actual relationship now. It's not just all about you anymore, and that kills you."

Conrad actually laughed. It was a bitter, terrible sound. "That's such BS." He turned to me. "Belly, are you hearing this? Jeremiah thinks I'm jealous."

Jeremiah looked at me, like, *Be on my side,* and I knew that if I did, he'd forgive me for not telling him about the house. I hated Conrad for putting me in the middle, for making me choose. I didn't know whose side I was on. They were both right and they were both wrong.

I guess I took too long to answer, because Jeremiah stopped looking at me and said, "You're an asshole, Conrad. You just want everyone to be as miserable as you are." And then he walked out. The front door slammed behind him.

I felt like I should go after him. I felt like I had just let him down when he needed me most.

Then Conrad said to me, "Am I an asshole, Belly?" He popped open another beer and he was trying to sound so indifferent, but his hand was shaking.

"Yeah," I said. "You really are."

I walked over to the window and I watched Jeremiah getting into his car. It was too late to follow him; he was already pulling out of the driveway. Even though he was pissed, he had his seat belt on.

"He'll be back," Conrad said.

I hesitated and then I said, "You shouldn't have said that stuff."

"Maybe not."

"You shouldn't have asked me to keep it a secret from him."

Conrad shrugged like he was already over it, but then he looked back toward the window and I knew he was worried. He threw me a beer and I caught it. I popped the top off and took a long drink. It hardly even tasted bad. Maybe I was getting used to it. I smacked my lips loudly.

He watched me, and there was a funny look on his face. "So you like beer now, huh?"

I shrugged. "It's all right," I said, and I felt very grown-up. But then I added, "I still like Cherry Coke better though."

He almost smiled when he said, "Same old Belly. I bet if we cut your body open, white sugar would come pouring out of you."

"That's me," I said. "Sugar and spice and everything nice."

Conrad said, "I don't know about that."

And then we were both quiet. I took another sip of beer and set it down next to Conrad. "I think you really hurt Jeremiah's feelings."

He shrugged. "He needed a reality check."

"You didn't have to do it like that."

"I think you're the one who hurt Jeremiah's feelings."

I opened my mouth and then closed it. If I asked him what he meant by that, he'd tell me. And I didn't want him to. So I drank my beer and said, "What now?"

Conrad didn't let me off the hook that easy. He said, "What now with you and Jeremiah or with you and me?"

He was teasing me and I hated him for it. I could feel my cheeks burning as I said, "What now with this house, was what I meant."

He leaned back against the counter. "There's nothing to do, really. I mean, I could get a lawyer. I'm eighteen now. I could try and stall. But I doubt it would do anything. My dad's stubborn. And he's greedy."

Hesitantly, I said, "I don't know that he's doing it out of—out of greed, Conrad."

Conrad's face sort of closed off. "Trust me. He is."

I couldn't help but ask, "What about summer school?"

"I couldn't care less about school right now."

"But—"

"Just leave it, Belly." Then he walked out of the kitchen, opened the sliding door, and went outside.

Conversation over.

chapter *twenty-six*
JEREMIAH

My whole life I've looked up to Conrad. He's always been smarter, faster—just better. The thing is, I never really begrudged him that. He was just Conrad. He couldn't help being good at things. He couldn't help that he never lost in Uno or races or grades. Maybe part of me needed that, someone to look up to. My big brother, the guy who couldn't lose.

But there was this time, when I was thirteen. We were wrestling around in the living room, had been for half an hour. My dad was always trying to get us to wrestle. He'd been on the wrestling team in college, and he liked teaching us new techniques. We were wrestling, and my mom was in the kitchen, cooking bacon-wrapped scallops because we were having people over that night and they were my dad's favorite.

"Lock him in, Con," my dad was saying.

We were really getting into it. We'd already knocked over one of my mom's silver candlesticks. Conrad was breathing hard; he'd expected to beat me easily. But I was getting good; I wasn't giving up. He had my head locked under his arm and then I locked his knee and we were both on the ground. I could feel something shift; I almost had him. I was going to win. My dad was gonna be so proud.

When I had him pinned, my dad said, "Connie, I told you to keep your knees bent."

I looked up at my dad, and I saw the look on his face. He had that look he got sometimes when Conrad wasn't doing something right, all tight around the eyes and irritated. He never looked at me like that.

He didn't say, "Good job, Jere." He just started criticizing Conrad, telling him all the things he could've done better. And Conrad took it. He was nodding, his face red, sweat pouring down his forehead. Then he nodded at me and said, in a way that I knew he really meant it, "Good job, Jere."

That's when my dad chimed in and said, "Yeah, good job, Jere."

All of a sudden, I wanted to cry. I didn't want to beat Conrad ever again. It wasn't worth it.

After all that stuff back at the house, I got in my car and I just started driving. I didn't know where I was going and part of me didn't even want to go back. Part of me wanted to leave Conrad to deal with this shitstorm by himself, the way he'd wanted it in the first place. Let Belly deal with him. Let them have at it. I drove for half an hour.

But even as I was doing it, I knew that, eventually, I would turn back around. I couldn't just leave. That was Con's style, not mine. And it *was* low, what I said about him not being there for our mom. It wasn't like he knew she was gonna die. He was at college. It wasn't his fault. But he wasn't the one who was there when everything got bad again. It all happened so fast. He couldn't have known. If he had known, he would have stayed home. I know he would have.

Our dad was never gonna win a Father of the Year award. He was flawed, that was for sure. But when it counted, there at the end, he came home. He said all the right things. He made our mom happy. Conrad just couldn't see it. He didn't want to.

I didn't go back to the house right away.

First I stopped at the pizza place. It was dinnertime, and there wasn't any food at the house. A kid I knew, Mikey, was working the register. I ordered a large pizza with everything, and then I asked him if Ron was out on a delivery. Mikey said yeah, that Ron would be back soon, that I should wait.

Ron lived in Cousins year-round. He went to community college during the day and he delivered pizzas at night. He was an okay guy. He'd been buying underage kids beer for as long as I could remember. If you gave him a twenty, he'd hook you up.

All I knew was, if this was gonna be our last night, we couldn't go out like this.

When I got back to the house, Conrad was sitting on the front porch. I knew he was waiting for me; I knew he felt bad for what he'd said. I honked the horn, stuck my head out the window, and yelled, "Come help me with this stuff."

He came down to the car, checked out the cases of beer and the bag of liquor, and said, "Ron?"

"Yup." I hoisted up two cases of beer and handed them over. "We're having a party."

chapter *twenty-seven*

After the fight, after Mr. Fisher left, I went up to my room and stayed there. I didn't want to be around when Jeremiah got back, in case he and Conrad went for a second round. Unlike Steven and me, those two hardly ever fought. In all the time I'd known them, I'd only seen them do it, like, three times. Jeremiah looked up to Conrad and Conrad looked out for Jeremiah. It was as simple as that.

I started looking around in the drawers and closet to see if there was anything of mine left there. My mom was pretty strict about us taking all our stuff every time we left, but you never knew. I figured I might as well make sure. Mr. Fisher would probably just tell the movers to throw all the junk out.

In the bottom of the desk drawer I found an old

composition notebook from my *Harriet the Spy* days. It was colored in pink and green and yellow highlighter. I'd followed the boys around for days, taking notes in it until I drove Steven crazy and he told Mom on me.

I'd written:

June 28. Caught Jeremiah dancing in the mirror when he thought no one was watching. Too bad I was!

June 30. Conrad ate all the blue Popsicles again even though he's not supposed to. But I didn't tell.

July 1. Steven kicked me for no reason.

And on and on. I'd gotten sick of it by mid-July and quit. I had been such a little tagalong then. Eight-year-old me would have loved to have been included in this last adventure, would have loved the fact that I got to hang out with the boys while Steven had to stay at home.

I found a few other things, junk like a half-used pot of cherry lip gloss, a couple of dusty hair bands. On the shelf, there were my old Judy Blumes and then my V. C. Andrews books hidden behind them. I figured I'd just leave all that stuff behind.

The one thing I had to take was Junior Mint, my old stuffed polar bear, the one Conrad had won me that time at the boardwalk a million years ago. I couldn't just let Junior Mint get thrown out like he was junk. He'd been special to me once upon a time.

I stayed upstairs for a while, just looking at my old stuff. I found one other thing worth keeping. A toy telescope. I remember the day my father bought it for me. It had been in one of the little antique stores along the boardwalk, and it was expensive but he said I should have it. There was a time when I was obsessed with stars and comets and constellations, and he thought I might grow up to be an astronomer. It turned out to be a phase, but it was fun while it lasted. I liked the way my father looked at me then, like I had taken after him, my father's daughter.

He still looked at me that way sometimes—when I asked for Tabasco sauce at restaurants, when I turned the radio station to NPR without him having to ask. Tabasco sauce I liked, but NPR not as much. I did it because I knew it made him proud.

I was glad he was my dad and not Mr. Fisher. He never would have yelled or cussed at me, or gotten mad about spilled Kool-Aid. He wasn't that kind of man. I'd never appreciated enough just what kind of man he was.

chapter *twenty-eight*

My father rarely came to the summer house, for a weekend in August maybe, but that was pretty much it. It never occurred to me to wonder why. There was this one weekend he and Mr. Fisher came up at the same time. As if they had so much in common, as if they were friends or something. They couldn't be more different. Mr. Fisher liked to talk, talk, talk, and my dad only spoke if he had something to say. Mr. Fisher was always watching SportsCenter, while my dad rarely watched TV at all—and definitely not sports.

The parents were going to a fancy restaurant in Dyerstown. A band played there on Saturday nights and they had a little dance floor. It was strange to think of my parents dancing. I'd never seen them dance before, but I was sure Susannah and Mr. Fisher danced all the time. I'd seen them once, in the living room. I remembered how Conrad had blushed and turned away.

I was lying on my stomach, on Susannah's bed, watching my mother and her get ready in the master bathroom.

Susannah had convinced my mother to wear a dress of hers; it was red and it had a deep V-neck. "What do you think, Beck?" my mother asked uncertainly. I could tell she felt funny about it. She usually wore pants.

"I think you look amazing. I think you should keep it. Red is so you, Laure." Susannah was curling her lashes and opening her eyes wide in the mirror.

When they left, I would practice using the eyelash curler. My mother didn't have one. I knew the contents of her makeup bag, one of those plastic green Clinique gift-with-purchase bags. It had a Burt's Bees chapstick and an espresso eyeliner, a pink and green tube of Maybelline mascara, and a bottle of tinted sunscreen. Boring.

Susannah's makeup case, though, was a treasure trove. It was a navy snakeskin case with a heavy gold clasp and her initials were engraved on it. Inside she had little eye pots and palettes and sable brushes and perfume samples. She never threw away anything. I liked to sort through it and organize everything in neat rows, according to color. Sometimes she gave me a lipstick or a sample eyeshadow, nothing too dark.

"Belly, you want me to do your eyes?" Susannah asked me.

I sat up. "Yeah!"

"Beck, please don't give her hooker eyes again," my mother said, running a comb through her wet hair.

Susannah made a face. "It's called a smoky eye, Laure."

"Yeah, Mom, it's a smoky eye," I piped up.

Susannah crooked her finger at me. "C'mere, Belly."

I scampered into the bathroom and propped myself up on the counter. I loved to sit on that counter with my legs dangling, listening in on everything like one of the girls.

She dipped a little brush into a pot of black eyeliner. "Close your eyes," she said.

I obeyed, and Susannah dragged the brush along my lash line, expertly blending and smudging with the ball of her thumb. Then she swept shadow across my eyelids and I wriggled in my seat excitedly. I loved it when Susannah made me up; I couldn't wait for the moment of unveiling.

"Are you and Mr. Fisher gonna dance tonight?" I asked.

Susannah laughed. "I don't know. Maybe."

"Mom, will you and Dad?"

My mother laughed too. "I don't know. Probably not. Your father doesn't like to dance."

"Dad's boring," I said, trying to twist around and get a peek at my new look. Gently, Susannah put her hands on my shoulders and sat me straight.

"He's not boring," my mother said. "He just has different interests. You like it when he teaches you the constellations, don't you?"

I shrugged. "Yeah."

"And he's very patient, and he always listens to your stories," my mother reminded me.

"True. But what does that have to do with being boring?"

"Not much, I suppose. But it has to do with being a good father, which I think he is."

"He definitely is," Susannah agreed, and she and my mother exchanged a look over my head. "Take a look at yourself."

I swiveled around and looked in the mirror. My eyes were very smoky and gray and mysterious. I felt like I should be the one going out dancing.

"See, she doesn't look like a hooker," Susannah said triumphantly.

"She looks like she has a black eye," my mother said.

"No, I don't. I look mysterious. I look like a countess." I hopped off the bathroom counter. "Thanks, Susannah."

"Anytime, sugar."

We air-kissed like two ladies who lunch. Then she took me by the hand and walked me over to her bureau. She handed me her jewelry box and said, "Belly, you have the best taste. Will you help me pick out some jewelry to wear tonight?"

I sat on her bed with the wooden box and sifted through it carefully. I found what I was looking for—her dangly opal earrings with the matching opal ring. "Wear these," I said, holding the jewelry out to her in the palm of my hand.

Susannah obeyed, and as she fastened the earrings, my mother said, "I don't know if that really goes."

In retrospect, I don't think it really did go. But I loved that opal jewelry so much. I admired it more than anything. So I said, "Mom, what do you know about style?"

Right away, I worried she'd be mad, but it had slipped out, and it was true after all. My mother knew about as much about jewelry as she did about makeup.

But Susannah laughed, and so did my mother.

"Go downstairs and tell the men we'll be ready to go in five, Countess," my mother ordered.

I jumped out of bed and curtsied dramatically. "Yes, Mum."

They both laughed. My mother said, "Go, you little imp."

I ran downstairs. When I was a kid, anytime I had to go anywhere, I ran. "They're almost ready," I yelled.

Mr. Fisher was showing my dad his new fishing rod. My dad looked relieved to see me, and he said, "Belly, what have they done to you?"

"Susannah made me up. Do you like it?"

My dad beckoned me closer, regarding me with serious eyes. "I'm not sure. You look very mature."

"I do?"

"Yes, very, very mature."

I tried to hide my delight as I made a place for myself in the crook of my dad's arm, my head right by his side. For me, there was no better compliment than being called mature.

They all left a little while later, the dads in pressed khakis and button-down shirts and the moms in their summer dresses. Mr. Fisher and my dad didn't look so different when they dressed up like that. My dad hugged me good-bye and said that if I was still awake when they got back, we'd sit on the deck awhile and look for shooting stars. My mother said they'd probably be back too late, but my dad winked at me.

On the way out, he whispered something to my mother that made her cover her mouth and laugh a low, throaty kind of laugh. I wonder what he said.

It was one of the last times I remember them being happy. I really wish I had enjoyed it more.

My parents had always been stable, as boring as two parents could be. They never fought. Taylor's parents fought all the time. I'd be over for a sleepover, and Mr. Jewel would come home late and her mom would be really pissy, stomping around in her slippers and banging pots. We'd be at the dinner table, and I would sink lower and lower into my seat, and Taylor would just go on talking about stupid stuff. Like whether or not Veronika Gerard wore the same socks two days in a row in gym or if we should volunteer to be water girls for the JV football team when we were freshmen.

When her parents got divorced, I asked Taylor if, in some little way, she was relieved. She said no. She said that even though they had fought all the time, at least they had still been a family. "Your parents never even fought," she said, and I could hear the disdain in her voice.

I knew what she meant. I wondered about it too. How could two people who had once been passionately in love not even fight? Didn't they care enough to fight it out, to fight not just with each other, but also for their marriage? Were they ever really in love? Did my mother ever feel about my dad the way I felt about Conrad— alive, crazy, drunk with tenderness? Those were the questions that haunted me.

I didn't want to make the same mistakes my parents made. I didn't want my love to fade away one day like an old scar. I wanted it to burn forever.

chapter *twenty-nine*

When I finally went back downstairs, it was dark out and Jeremiah was back. He and Conrad were sitting on the couch, watching TV like the fight had never happened. I guessed it was that way with boys. Whenever Taylor and I fought, we were mad for at least a week and there was a power struggle over who got custody of which friends. "Whose side are you on?" we'd demand of Katie or Marcy. We'd say mean things that you can't take back and then we'd cry and make up. Somehow I doubted Conrad and Jeremiah had been crying and making up while I'd been upstairs.

I wondered if I was forgiven too, for keeping a secret from Jeremiah, for not taking a side—his side. Because it was true, we'd come here together as partners, a team, and when he'd needed me, I'd let him down. I lingered there by the stairs for a second, unsure of whether or not to go over, and then Jeremiah looked up at me and I knew I was. Forgiven, that is. He smiled, a real smile, and a real Jeremiah smile was the kind that could melt ice cream. I smiled back, grateful as anything.

"I was just about to come get you," he said. "We're having a party."

There was a pizza box on the coffee table. "A pizza party?" I asked.

Susannah used to have pizza parties for us kids all the time. It was never just "pizza for dinner." It was a pizza party. Except this time, with beer. And tequila. So this was it. Our last night. It would have felt a lot more real if Steven had been there too. It would have felt complete, us four together again.

"I ran into some people in town. They're gonna come over later and bring a keg."

"A keg?" I repeated.

"Yeah. A keg, you know, of beer?"

"Oh, right," I said. "A keg."

Then I sat down on the ground and opened the pizza box. There was one slice left, and it was a small one. "You guys are such pigs," I said, stuffing it into my mouth.

"Whoops, sorry," Jeremiah said. Then he went into the kitchen, and when he came back, he had three cups. He had one balanced in the crook of his elbow. He gave that one to me. "Cheers," he said. He handed Conrad a cup too.

I sniffed it suspiciously. It was light brown with a lime wedge floating on top. "Smells strong," I said.

"That's because it's *tequila*," he sang. He lifted his cup in the air. "To the last night."

"To the last night," we repeated.

They both drank theirs in one shot. I took a teeny sip of mine, and it wasn't too bad. I'd never had tequila before. I drank the rest quickly. "This is pretty good," I said. "Not strong at all."

Jeremiah burst out laughing. "That's because yours is ninety-five percent water."

Conrad laughed too, and I glared at them both. "That's not fair," I said. "I want to drink what you guys are drinking."

"Sorry, but we don't serve minors here," Jeremiah said, falling next to me on the floor.

I punched him on the shoulder. "You're a minor too, dummy. We all are."

"Yeah, but you're really a minor," he said. "My mom would kill me."

It was the first time any of us had mentioned Susannah. My eyes darted over to Conrad, but his face was blank. I let out a breath. And then I had an idea, the best idea ever. I jumped up and opened the doors of the TV console. I ran my fingers along the drawers of DVDs and home videos, all neatly labeled in Susannah's slanted cursive handwriting. I found what I was looking for.

"What are you doing?" Jeremiah asked me.

"Just wait," I said, my back to them. I turned on the TV and popped in the video.

On the screen, there was Conrad, age twelve. With braces and bad skin. He was lying on a beach blanket, scowling. He wouldn't let anybody take a picture of him that summer.

Mr. Fisher was behind the camera, as always, saying, "Come on. Say 'Happy Fourth of July,' Connie."

Jeremiah and I looked at each other and burst out laughing. Conrad glared at us. He made a move for the remote, but Jeremiah got to it first. He held it above his head, laughing breathlessly. The two of them started wrestling around, and then they stopped.

The camera had focused in on Susannah, wearing her big beach hat and a long white shirt over her bathing suit.

"Suze, honey, how do you feel today, on our nation's birthday?"

She rolled her eyes. "Give it a rest, Adam. Go videotape the kids." And then from under her hat, she smiled—that slow, deep-down smile. It was the smile of a woman who really and truly loved the person holding the video camera.

Conrad stopped fighting for the remote and he watched for a moment, then he said, "Turn it off."

Jeremiah said, "Come on, man. Let's just watch."

Conrad didn't say anything but he didn't stop watching either.

And then the camera was on me, and Jeremiah was laughing again. Conrad too. This was what I was waiting for. I knew it would get a laugh.

Me, wearing huge glasses and a rainbow striped tankini, my round stomach popping over the bottoms like a four-year-old's. I was screaming at the top of my lungs, running away from Steven and Jeremiah. They were chasing me with what they claimed was a jellyfish, but what I later found out was a clump of seaweed.

Jeremiah's hair was white-blond in the sunlight, and he looked exactly the way I remembered.

"Bells, you look like a beach ball," he said, gasping with laughter.

I laughed too, a little. "Watch it," I said. "That summer was really great. All our summers here were really . . . great."

Great didn't even begin to describe them.

Silently, Conrad got up and then he came back with the tequila. He poured us each some, and this time mine wasn't watered down.

We all took a shot together, and when I gulped mine down it burned so bad tears streamed down my face. Conrad and Jeremiah started cracking up again. "Suck on the lime," Conrad told me, so I did.

Soon I felt warm and lazy and great. I lay down on the floor with my hair fanned out and I stared up at the ceiling and watched the fan turn round and round.

When Conrad got up and went to the bathroom,

Jeremiah rolled over to his side. "Hey, Belly," he said. "Truth or dare."

"Don't be dumb," I said.

"Oh, come on. Play with me, Bells. Please?"

I rolled my eyes and sat up. "Dare."

His eyes had that trickster's glint. I hadn't seen that look in his eyes since before Susannah got sick again. "I dare you to kiss me, old-school style. I've learned a lot since the last time."

I laughed. Whatever I had been expecting him to say, it hadn't been that.

Jeremiah tilted his face up at me and I laughed again. I leaned forward, pulled his chin toward me, and kissed him on the cheek with a loud smack.

"Aw, man!" he protested. "That's not a real kiss."

"You didn't specify," I said, and my face felt hot.

"Come on, Bells," he said. "That's not how we kissed that other time."

Conrad came back into the room then, wiping his hands on his jeans. He said, "What are you talking about, Jere? Don't you have a girlfriend?"

I looked at Jeremiah, whose cheeks were flaming. "You have a girlfriend?" I heard the accusation in my voice and I hated it. It wasn't like Jeremiah owed me anything. It wasn't like he belonged to me. But he always let me feel like he did.

All this time together, and he never once mentioned

that he had a girlfriend. I couldn't believe it. I guessed I wasn't the only one keeping secrets, and the thought made me sad.

"We broke up. She's going to school at Tulane, and I'm staying around here. We decided there's no point in staying together." He glared at Conrad and then glanced back at me. "And we've always been off and on. She's crazy."

I hated the idea of him with some crazy girl, some girl who he liked enough to go back to over and over. "Well, what's her name?" I asked.

He hesitated. "Mara," he said at last.

The alcohol in me gave me the courage to say, "Do you love her?"

This time he didn't hesitate. "No," he said.

I picked at a pizza crust and said, "Okay, my turn. Conrad, truth or dare?"

He was lying on the couch facedown. "Never said I was playing."

"Chicken," Jeremiah and I said together.

"Jinx," we said at the same time.

"You guys are two-year-olds," Conrad muttered.

Jeremiah got up and started doing his chicken dance. "Bock bock bock bock."

"Truth or dare," I repeated.

Conrad groaned. "Truth."

I was so pleased Conrad was playing with us, I couldn't think of anything good to ask. I mean, there were a million and one things I wanted to ask him. I wanted to ask him what had happened to us, if he'd ever liked me, if any of it had been real. But I couldn't ask those things. Even through my tequila haze, I knew that much.

Instead, I asked, "Remember that summer you liked that girl who worked at the boardwalk? Angie?"

"No," he said, but I knew he was lying. "What about her?"

"Did you ever hook up with her?"

Conrad finally lifted his head up from the couch. "No," he said.

"I don't believe you."

"I tried, once. But she socked me in the head and said she wasn't that kind of girl. I think she was a Jehovah's Witness or something."

Jeremiah and I busted up laughing. Jeremiah was laughing so hard, he doubled over and fell to his knees. "Oh, man," he gasped. "That's awesome."

And it was. I knew it was only because he'd had about a case of beer, but Conrad loosening up, telling us things—it felt awesome. Like a miracle.

Conrad propped himself up on his elbow. "Okay. My turn."

He was looking at me like we were the only two people in the room, and suddenly I was terrified. And elated. But then I looked over at Jeremiah, watching the two of us, and just as suddenly, I was neither.

Solemnly I said, "Nuh-uh. You can't ask me, 'cause I just asked you. It's the law."

"The law?" he repeated.

"Yeah," I said, leaning my head against the couch.

"Aren't you at least curious about what I was going to ask?"

"Nope. Not even one iota." Which was a lie. Of course I was curious. I was dying to know.

I reached over and poured some more tequila into my cup and then I stood up, my knees shaking. I felt light-headed. "To our last night!"

"We already toasted to that, remember?" Jeremiah said.

I stuck my tongue out at him. "Okay, then." The tequila made me feel brave again. This time, it let me say what I really wanted to say. What I'd been thinking all night. "Here's to . . . here's to everybody that isn't here tonight. To my mom, and to Steven, and to Susannah most of all. Okay?"

Conrad looked up at me. For a minute, I was afraid of what he would say. And then he lifted his cup too, and so did Jeremiah. We all swigged from our cups together, and it burned like liquid fire. I coughed a little.

When I sat back down I asked Jeremiah, "So, who's coming to this party?"

He shrugged. "Some kids from the country club pool from last summer. They're telling people too. Oh, and Mikey and Pete and those guys."

I wondered who "Mikey and Pete and those guys" were. I also wondered if I should clean up before people came.

"What time are people coming over?" I asked Jeremiah.

He shrugged. "Ten? Eleven?"

I jumped up. "It's already almost nine! I have to get dressed."

Conrad said, "Aren't you already dressed?"

I didn't even bother to answer him. I just shot upstairs.

chapter *thirty*

I had the contents of my duffel bag dumped out on the floor when Taylor called. Which was when I remembered that it was Saturday. It felt like I'd been gone much longer. Then I remembered that it was the Fourth of July. And I was supposed to be on a boat with Taylor and Davis and everyone. *Gulp.*

"Hey, Taylor," I said.

"Hey, where are you?" Taylor didn't sound mad, which was kind of freaky.

"Um, still in Cousins. Sorry I didn't make it back in time for the boat party." From the pile of clothes, I picked out a chiffony one-shoulder blouse and tried it on. Whenever Taylor wore it, she wore her hair pulled to the side.

"It's been raining all day, so we cancelled the boat

party. Cory's having a party tonight at his brother's condo instead. What about you?"

"I think we're having a party too. Jeremiah just bought a ton of beer and tequila and stuff," I said, adjusting the blouse. I wasn't sure how much shoulder I was supposed to be showing.

"A party?" she squealed. "I wanna come!"

I tried to wiggle my foot into one of Taylor's platform sandals. I wished I hadn't mentioned the party—or the tequila. Lately, Taylor was crazy for tequila body shots. "What about Cory's party?" I said. "I heard his brother's condo has a Jacuzzi. You love Jacuzzis."

"Oh, yeah. Darn. But I want to party with you guys too! Beach parties are the funnest," she said. "Anyway, I heard from Rachel Spiro that a bunch of freshman sluts are coming now. It might not even be worth it to go. OMG, maybe I should just get in my car and drive to Cousins!"

"By the time you got here, everybody would be gone. You should probably just go to Cory's."

I heard a car pull into the driveway. People were already here. So it wasn't like I was lying to her.

I was about to tell Taylor I had to go when she said in a little voice, "Do you, like, not want me to come?"

"I didn't say that," I said.

"You basically did."

"Taylor," I began. But I didn't know what to say next. Because she was right. I didn't want her to come. If she came, it would be all about her, the way it always was. This was my last night in Cousins, in this house. I was never going to be inside this house again, ever. I wanted tonight to be about me and Conrad and Jeremiah.

Taylor waited for me to say something, to deny it at least, and when I didn't, she spat out, "I can't even believe how selfish you are, Belly."

"Me?"

"Yes, you. You keep your summer house and your summer boys all to yourself and you don't want to share anything with me. We finally get to spend a whole summer together and you don't even care! All you care about is being in Cousins, with *them*." She sounded so spiteful. But instead of feeling guilty the way I normally would, I just felt annoyed.

"Taylor," I said.

"Quit saying my name like that."

"Like how?"

"Like I'm a child."

"Well, then maybe you shouldn't act like one just because you aren't invited somewhere." As soon as I said it, I regretted it.

"Screw you, Belly! I put up with a lot. You are a really crappy best friend, you know that?"

I let out a breath. "Taylor . . . shut up."

She gasped. "Don't you dare tell me to shut up! I have been nothing but supportive of you, Belly. I listen to all your Conrad BS and I don't even complain. When you guys broke up, who was the one who spoon-fed you Chunky Monkey and got you out of bed? Me! And you don't even appreciate that. You're, like, hardly even fun anymore."

Sarcastically, I said, "Gee, Taylor, I'm so sorry I'm not fun anymore. Having someone you love die can do that."

"Don't do that. Don't just blame it on that. You've been chasing after Conrad for as long as I've known you. It's getting pathetic. Get over it! He doesn't like you. Maybe he never did."

That was maybe the meanest thing she'd ever said to me. I think she might have apologized if I hadn't come back at her with, "At least I didn't give away my virginity to a guy who shaves his legs!"

She gasped. In confidence, Taylor had once told me that Davis shaved his legs for swim team. She was silent for a moment. And then she said, "You better not wear my platforms tonight."

"Too late. I already am!" And then I hung up.

I couldn't believe her. Taylor was the crappy friend, not me. She was the selfish one. I was so angry, my hand shook when I put on my eyeliner and I had to rub it off and start over again. I wore Taylor's blouse and her shoes and I pulled my hair all to one side too. I did it because I knew it would piss her off.

And then, last of all, I put on Conrad's necklace. I tucked it underneath my shirt, and then I went downstairs.

chapter *thirty-one*

"Welcome," I said to a boy in a Led Zeppelin T-shirt.

"Nice boots," I said to a girl with cowboy boots on.

I made my way around the room, passing out drinks and throwing away empty cans. Conrad watched me with his arms crossed. "What are you doing?" he asked me.

"I'm trying to make everyone feel at home," I explained, adjusting Taylor's top. Susannah was an excellent hostess. She had a talent for making people feel welcome, wanted. Taylor's words were still hanging around in the back of my head. I wasn't selfish. I was a good friend, a good hostess. I'd show her.

When Travis from Video World put his feet up on the coffee table and almost knocked over a hurricane vase, I barked, "Careful. And take your feet off the furniture." As an afterthought, I added, "Please."

I was about to go back into the kitchen for more drinks when I saw her. The girl from last summer. Nicole, the one Conrad liked, was standing in the kitchen talking to Jeremiah. She didn't have her Red Sox hat on, but I'd recognize her perfume anywhere. It smelled like vanilla extract and decomposing roses.

Conrad must have seen her at the same time I did because he sucked in his breath and muttered, "*Shit.*"

"Did you break her heart?" I asked him. I tried to sound teasing and carefree.

I must have succeeded, because he took me by the hand and grabbed the bottle of tequila and said, "Let's get out of here."

I followed him like I was in a trance, sleepwalking. Because it was like a dream, his hand in mine. We were almost home free when Jeremiah saw us. My heart just sank. He motioned us over and called out, "Guys! Come say hi."

Conrad let go of my hand but not the tequila. "Hey, Nicole," he said, starting toward her. I grabbed a couple of beers and followed him over.

"Oh, hey, Conrad," Nicole said, all surprised, like she hadn't been watching the whole time we'd been in the kitchen. She got on her tip-toes and hugged him.

Jeremiah caught my eye and raised his eyebrows comically. He grinned at me. "Belly, you remember Nicole, right?"

I said, "Of course." I smiled at her. *Perfect hostess*, I reminded myself. *Unselfish.*

Warily, she smiled back at me. I handed her one of the beers I was holding. "Cheers," I said, opening mine.

"Cheers," she echoed. We clinked cans and drank. I drank mine fast. When I was done, I got another and I drank that, too.

Suddenly the house felt too quiet, so I turned on the stereo. I turned the music up loud and kicked off my shoes. Susannah always said it wasn't a party without dancing. I grabbed Jeremiah, threw one arm around his neck, and danced.

"Belly—," he protested.

"Just dance, Jere!" I yelled.

So he did. He was a good dancer, that Jeremiah. Other people started dancing too, even Nicole. Not Conrad though, but I didn't care. I barely even noticed.

I danced like it was 1999. I danced like my heart was breaking, which it kind of was. Mostly I just swung my hair around a lot.

I was pretty sweaty when I said, "Can we swim in the pool? One last time?"

Jeremiah said, "Screw that. Let's swim in the ocean."

"Yeah!" It sounded like a great idea to me. A perfect idea.

"No," Conrad said, coming out of nowhere. He was suddenly standing right beside me. "Belly's drunk. She shouldn't swim."

I looked at him and frowned. "But I want to," I said.

He laughed. "So what?"

"Look, I'm a really good swimmer. And I'm not even drunk." I walked in a semistraight line to prove my point.

"Sorry," he said. "But you really are."

Dumb, boring Conrad. He got so serious at the worst moments.

"You're no fun." I looked over at Jeremiah, who was sitting on the floor now. "He's no fun. And he's not the boss of us. Right, everybody?"

Before Jeremiah or anybody else could answer me, I made a run for the sliding doors, and then I stumbled down the steps and sprinted onto the beach. I felt like a flying comet, a streak in the sky, like I hadn't used my muscles in so long and it felt great to stretch my legs and *run*.

The house, all lit up with people inside, felt a million miles away. I knew he'd come after me. I didn't have to turn around to know it was him. But I did anyway.

"Come back to the house," Conrad said. He had the bottle of tequila in his hand. I grabbed it out of his hand and took a swig like I'd done it a million times before, like I was the kind of girl who could drink right from the bottle.

I was proud of myself for not spitting it back up. I took a step toward the water, smiling big at him. I was testing him.

"Belly," he warned. "I'm telling you now, I'm not

going to pull your dead body out of the ocean when you drown."

I crossed my eyes at him and then I dipped my toe in. The water was colder than I'd thought it'd be. Suddenly swimming didn't sound like such a great idea. But I hated backing down to Conrad. I hated losing to him. "Are you gonna stop me?"

He sighed and looked back toward the house.

I continued, took another glug of tequila. Anything to make him pay attention. "I mean, 'cause I am a stronger swimmer than you. I'm way, way faster. You probably couldn't catch me if you wanted to."

He was looking at me again. "I'm not coming after you."

"Really? You really aren't?" I took a big step, then another. The water was up to my knees. It was low tide, and I was shivering. It was stupid, really. I didn't even want to swim anymore. I didn't know what I was doing. Far down on the other side of the beach, somebody shot off a firecracker. It sounded like a missile. It looked like a silver weeping willow. I watched it drop down into the ocean.

And just when I started to feel disappointed, just when I'd resigned myself to the fact that he didn't care, he moved toward me. He heaved me up, over his shoulder. I dropped the bottle right into the ocean.

"Put me down!" I screamed, pounding on his back.

"Belly, you're drunk."

"Put me down right now!"

And for once, he actually listened. He dropped me, right in the sand, right on my butt. "Ow! That really hurt!"

It didn't hurt that bad, but I was mad, and more than that, I was embarrassed. I kicked sand at his back and the wind kicked it right back at me. "Jerk!" I yelled, sputtering and spitting out sand.

Conrad shook his head and turned away from me. His jeans were wet. He was leaving. He was really leaving. I'd ruined everything again.

When I stood up I felt so dizzy I almost fell right back down.

"Wait," I said, and my knees wobbled. I pushed my sandy hair out of my face and took a deep breath. I had to say it, had to tell him. My last chance.

He turned back around. His face was a closed door.

"Just wait a second, please. I need to tell you something. I'm really sorry for the way I acted that day." My voice was high and desperate, and I was crying, and I hated that I was crying, but I couldn't help it. I had to keep talking, because this was it. Last chance. "At . . . at the funeral, I was awful to you. I was horrible, and I'm so ashamed of how I acted. It wasn't how I wanted things to go, not at all. I really, really wanted to be there for you. That's why I came to find you."

Conrad blinked once and then again. "It's fine."

I wiped my cheeks and my runny nose. I said, "Do you mean it? You forgive me?"

"Yes," he said. "I forgive you. Now stop crying, all right?"

I stepped toward him, closer and closer still, and he didn't back away. We were close enough to kiss. I was holding my breath, wanting so badly for things to be like before.

I took one step closer, and that's when he said, "Let's go back, okay?"

Conrad didn't wait for me to answer him. He just started walking away, and I followed. I felt like I was going to be sick.

Just like that, the moment was over. It was an almost moment, where almost anything could have happened. But he had made it be over.

Back at the house, people were swimming in the pool in their clothes. A few girls were waving sparklers around. Clay Bertolet, our neighbor, was floating along the edge of the pool in one of his undershirts. He grabbed my ankles. "Come on, Belly, swim with me," he said.

"Let go," I said, kicking him off and splashing his face in the process.

I pushed my way through all the people on the deck and made my way back into the house. I accidentally stepped on some girl's foot and she screamed. "Sorry," I said, and my voice came out sounding far away. I was so dizzy. I just wanted my bed.

I crawled up the stairs with my hands, like a crab, the way I used to when I was a little kid. I fell into bed, and it was just like they say in the movies, the room was spinning. The bed was spinning, and then I remembered all the stupid stuff I said, and I started to cry.

I made a real fool of myself out on that beach. It was devastating, all of it—Susannah gone, the thought of this house not being ours anymore, me giving Conrad the chance to reject me one more time. Taylor was right: I was a masochist.

I lay on my side and hugged my knees to my chest and wept. Everything was wrong, and most of all me. Suddenly I just wanted my mother.

I reached across the bed for the phone on my nightstand. The numbers lit up in the darkness. My mother picked up on the fourth ring.

Her voice was drowsy and familiar in a way that made me cry harder. More than anything in the world, I wanted to reach inside the phone and bring her here.

"Mommy," I said. My voice came out a croak.

"Belly? What's wrong? Where are you?"

"I'm at Susannah's. At the summer house."

"What? What are you doing at the summer house?"

"Mr. Fisher's gonna sell it. He's gonna sell it and Conrad is so sad and Mr. Fisher doesn't even care. He just wants to get rid of it. He wants to get rid of her."

"Belly, slow down. I can't hear what you're saying."

"Just come, okay? Just please come and fix it."

And then I hung up, because suddenly the phone felt very heavy in my hand. I felt like I was on a merry-go-round, and not in a good way. Somebody was setting off fireworks outside, and it felt like my head was pounding right along with them. Then I closed my eyes and it was worse. But my eyelids felt heavy too and soon I was asleep.

chapter *thirty-two*
JEREMIAH

Pretty soon after Belly went up to bed, I cleared everybody out and it was just Conrad and me. He was lying facedown on the couch. He'd been lying there since he and Belly came back from the beach. They were both wet and sandy. Belly was wasted, and she'd been crying, I could tell. Her eyes were red. Conrad's fault—no doubt about that.

People had tracked sand inside and it was all over the floor. There were bottles and cans everywhere, and somebody had sat on the couch in a wet towel, and now the cushion had a big orange spot. I flipped it over. "The house is a wreck," I said, falling onto the La-Z-Boy. "Dad will freak out if he sees it like this tomorrow."

Conrad didn't open his eyes. "Whatever. We'll clean it in the morning."

I stared at him, just feeling pissed. I was sick of cleaning up his messes. "It's gonna take us hours."

Then he opened his eyes. "You're the one who invited everybody over."

He had a point. The party had been my idea. It wasn't the mess I was pissed about. It was Belly. Him and her, together. It made me sick.

"Your jeans are wet," I said. "You're getting sand all over the couch."

Conrad sat up, rubbed his eyes. "What's your problem?"

I couldn't take it anymore. I started to get up, but then I sat back down. "What the hell happened outside with you guys?"

"Nothing."

"What does that mean, nothing?"

"Nothing means nothing. Just leave it, Jere."

I hated it when he got like that, all stoic and detached, especially when I was mad. He'd always been like that, but it was more and more these days. When our mom died, he changed. Conrad didn't give two shits about anything or anyone anymore. I wondered if that included Belly.

I had to know. About him and her, how he really felt, what he was going to do about it. It was the not knowing that killed a guy.

So I asked him flat out. "Do you still like her?"

He stared at me. I'd shocked the hell out of him, I could tell. We'd never talked about her before, not like this. It was probably a good thing that I'd caught him off guard. Maybe he'd tell the truth.

If he said yes, it was over. If he said yes, I would give her up. I could live with that. If it were anyone but Conrad, I'd have tried anyway. I'd have given it one last shot.

Instead of answering the question, he said, "Do you?"

I could feel myself turn red. "I'm not the one who took her to the freaking prom."

Conrad thought that over and then said, "I only took her because she asked me to."

"Con. Do you like her or not, man?" I hesitated for about two seconds, and then I just went for it. "Because I do. I like her. I really like her. Do you?"

He didn't blink, didn't even hesitate. "No."

It really pissed me off.

He was full of shit. He liked her. He more than liked her. But he couldn't admit it, wouldn't man up. Conrad would never be that guy, the kind of guy Belly needed. Someone who would be there for her, someone she could count on. I could. If she'd let me, I could be that guy.

I was pissed at him, but I had to admit I was relieved, too. No matter how many times he hurt her, I knew that if he wanted her back, she was his. She always had been.

But maybe now that Conrad wasn't standing in the way, she'd see me there too.

chapter *thirty-three*

JULY 5

"Belly."

I tried to roll over, but then I heard it again, louder.

"Belly!" Someone was shaking me awake.

I opened my eyes. It was my mother. She had dark circles around her eyes and her mouth had all but disappeared into a thin line. She was wearing her house sweats, the ones she never left the house in, not even to go to the gym. What in the world was she doing at the summer house?

There was a beeping sound that at first I thought was the alarm clock, but then I realized that I had knocked the phone over, and it was the busy signal I was hearing. And then I remembered. I'd drunk-dialed my mother. I'd brought her here.

I sat up, my head pounding so hard it felt like my heart

was hammering inside it. So this was what a hangover felt like. I'd left my contacts in and my eyes were burning. There was sand all over the bed and some was stuck on my feet.

My mother stood up; she was one big blur. "You have five minutes to pack up your stuff."

"Wait . . . what?"

"We're leaving."

"But I can't leave yet. I still have to—"

It was like she couldn't hear me, like I was on mute. She started picking my things up off the floor, throwing Taylor's sandals and shorts into my overnight bag.

"Mom, stop! Just stop for a minute."

"We're leaving in five minutes," she repeated, looking around the room.

"Just listen to me for a second. I had to come. Jeremiah and Conrad needed me."

The look on my mother's face made me stop short. I'd never seen her angry like this before.

"And you didn't feel the need to tell me about it? Beck asked me to look after her boys. How can I do that when I don't even know they need my help? If they were in trouble, you should have told me. Instead you chose to lie to me. You *lied*."

"I didn't want to lie to you—," I started to say.

She kept on going. "You've been here doing God knows what . . ."

I stared at her. I couldn't believe she'd just said that.

"What does that mean, 'God knows what'?"

My mother' whirled around, her eyes all wild. "What am I supposed to think? You snuck out here with Conrad before and you spent the night! So you tell me. What *are* you doing here with him? Because it looks to me like you lied to me so you could come here and get drunk and fool around with your boyfriend."

I hated her. I hated her so much.

"He's not my boyfriend! You don't know anything!"

The vein in my mother's forehead was pulsing. "You call me at four in the morning, drunk. I call your cell phone and it goes straight to voice mail. I call the house phone and all I get is a busy signal. I drive all night, worried out of my mind, and I get here and the house is a wreck. Beer cans everywhere, trash all over the place. What the hell do you think you're doing, Isabel? Or do you even know?"

The walls in the house were really thin. Everyone could probably hear everything.

I said, "We were going to clean it up. This was our last night here. Don't you get it? Mr. Fisher is selling the house. Don't you care?"

She shook her head, her jaw tight. "Do you really think you've helped matters by meddling? This isn't our business. How many times do I have to explain that to you?"

"It is so our business. Susannah would have wanted us to save this house!"

"Don't talk to me about what Susannah would have wanted," my mother snapped. "Now put your clothes on and get your things. We're leaving."

"No." I pulled the covers up to my shoulders.

"What?"

"I said no. I'm not going!" I stared up at my mother as defiantly as I could, but I could feel my chin trembling.

She marched over to the bed and ripped the sheets right off of me. She grabbed my arm, pulled me out of the bed and toward the door, and I twisted away from her.

"You can't make me go," I sobbed. "You can't tell me anything. You don't have the right."

My tears did not move my mother. They only made her angrier. She said, "You're acting like a spoiled brat. Can't you look beyond your own grief and think about someone else? It's not all about you. We all lost Beck. Feeling sorry for yourself isn't helping anything."

Her words stung me so badly I wanted to hurt her back a million times worse. So I said the thing I knew would hurt her most. I said, "I wish Susannah was my mother and not you."

How many times had I thought it, wished for it secretly? When I was little, Susannah was the one I ran to, not her. I used to wonder what it would be like, to have a mom like Susannah who loved me for me and wasn't disappointed in all the ways that I didn't measure up.

I was breathing hard as I waited for my mother to respond. To cry, to scream at me.

She didn't do either of those things. Instead she said, "How unfortunate for you."

Even when I tried my hardest, I couldn't get the reaction I wanted from my mother. She was impenetrable.

I said, "Susannah will never forgive you for this, you know. For losing her house. For letting down her boys."

My mother's hand reached out and struck my cheek so hard I rocked back. I didn't see it coming. I clutched my face and right away I cried, but part of me was satisfied. I finally got what I wanted. Proof that she could feel something.

Her face was white. She had never hit me before. Never ever, not in my whole life.

I waited for her to say she was sorry. To say she didn't mean to hurt me, she didn't mean the things she'd said. If she said those things, then I would say them too. Because I was sorry. I didn't mean the things I said.

When she didn't speak, I backed away from her and then around her, holding my face. Then I ran out of the room, stumbling over my feet.

Jeremiah was standing in the hallway, looking at me with his mouth open. He looked at me like he didn't recognize me, like he didn't know who this person was, this girl who screamed at her mother and said terrible things. "Wait," he said, reaching out to stop me.

I pushed past him and moved down the stairs.

In the living room, Conrad was picking up beer bottles and tossing them into a blue recycling bag. He didn't look at me. I knew he'd heard everything too.

I ran out the back door and then I almost tripped going down the stairs that headed down to the beach. I sank to the ground and sat in the sand, holding my burning cheek in the palm of my hand. And then I threw up.

I heard Jeremiah come up behind me. I knew it was him right away, because Conrad would know not to follow me.

"I just want to be alone," I said, wiping my mouth. I didn't turn around. I didn't want him to see my face.

"Belly," he started. He sat down next to me and kicked sand over my throw up.

When he didn't say anything more, I looked at him. "What?"

He bit his upper lip. Then he reached out and touched my cheek. His fingers felt warm. He looked so sad. He said, "You should just go with your mom."

Whatever I'd been expecting him to say, it hadn't been that. I'd come all this way and I'd gotten in so much trouble, just so I could help him and Conrad, and now he wanted me to leave? Tears welled up in the corners of my eyes and I wiped them away with the back of my hands. "Why?"

"Because Laurel's really upset. Everything's gone to

crap, and it's my fault. I never should have asked you to come. I'm sorry."

"I'm not leaving."

"Pretty soon we'll all have to."

"And that's it?"

He shrugged. "Yeah, I guess it is."

We sat in the sand for a while. I had never felt more lost. I cried a little more, and Jeremiah didn't say anything, which I was grateful for. There was nothing worse than your friend watching you cry after you just got in trouble with your mother. When I was done, he stood up and gave me his hand. "Come on," he said, pulling me to my feet.

We went back inside the house. Conrad was gone and the living room was clean. My mother was mopping the kitchen floor. When she saw me, she stopped. She put the mop back into the bucket and leaned it against the wall.

Right in front of Jeremiah, she said, "I'm sorry."

I looked at him, and he backed out of the kitchen and went up the stairs. I almost stopped him. I didn't want to be alone with her. I was afraid.

She continued. "You're right. I've been absent. I've been so consumed with my own grief, I haven't reached out to you. I'm sorry for that."

"Mom—," I started to say. I was about to tell her I was sorry too, for saying that thing before, that awful thing I wished I could take back. But she lifted her hand up and stopped me.

"I'm just—off balance. Ever since Beck died, I can't seem to find my equilibrium." She rested her head against the wall. "I've been coming here with Beck since I was younger than you are now. I love this house. You know that."

"I know," I said. "I didn't mean it, what I said before."

My mother nodded. "Let's sit down a minute, all right?"

She sat down at the kitchen table and I took a seat across from her.

"I shouldn't have hit you," she said, and her voice broke. "I'm sorry."

"You never did that before."

"I know."

My mother reached across the table and took my hand in hers, tight as a cocoon. At first I felt stiff, but then I let her comfort me. Because I could see it was a comfort to her, too. We sat like that for what felt like a long time.

When she let go, she said, "You lied to me, Belly. You never lie to me."

"I didn't mean to. But Conrad and Jeremiah are important to me. They needed me, so I went."

"I wish you would have told me. Beck's boys are important to me, too. If something's going on, I want to know about it. Okay?"

I nodded.

Then she said, "Are you all packed? I want to beat Sunday traffic on the way back."

I stared at her. "Mom, we can't just leave. Not with everything that's happening. You can't let Mr. Fisher sell the house. You just can't."

She sighed. "I don't know that I can say anything to change his mind, Belly. Adam and I don't see eye to eye on a lot of things. I can't stop him from selling the house if that's what he's set on."

"You can, I know you can. He'll listen to you. Conrad and Jeremiah, they need this house. They need it."

I set my head down on the table, and the wood was cool and smooth against my cheek. My mother touched the top of my head, running her hand through my tangled hair.

"I'll call him," she said at last. "Now get upstairs and take a shower." Hopefully, I looked up at her and I saw the firm set of her mouth and the narrow of her eyes. And I knew it wasn't over yet.

If anybody could make things right, it was my mother.

chapter *thirty-four*
JEREMIAH

There was this time—I think I was thirteen and Belly was eleven, about to turn twelve. She'd caught a summer cold, and she was miserable. She was camped out on the couch with balled-up tissues all around her, and she'd been wearing the same ratty pajamas for days. Because she was sick, she got to pick whatever TV show she wanted to watch. The only thing she could eat were grape Popsicles, and when I reached for one, my mother said that Belly should have it. Even though she'd already had three. I got stuck with a yellow one.

It was afternoon, and Conrad and Steven had hitch-hiked to the arcade, which I wasn't supposed to know about. The moms thought they were riding their bikes to the tackle shop for more rubber worms. I was going to go boarding with Clay, and I had my swim trunks on and a towel around my neck when I ran into my mom in the kitchen.

"What are you up to, Jere?" she asked.

I made a hang ten sign. "I'm gonna go boarding with Clay. See ya!"

I was about to push the sliding door open when she said, "Hmm. You know what?"

Suspiciously, I asked, "What?"

"It might be nice if you stayed inside today and cheered up Belly. Poor thing could use some cheering up."

"Aw, Mom—"

"Please, Jeremiah?"

I sighed. I didn't want to stay home and cheer up Belly. I wanted to go boarding with Clay.

When I didn't say anything, she added, "We can grill out tonight. I'll let you be in charge of the burgers."

I sighed again, louder this time. My mom still thought that letting me fire up the grill and flip hamburgers was a big treat for me. Not that it wasn't fun, but still. I opened my mouth to say "no thanks," but then I saw the fond, happy look on her face, the way she just knew I would say yes. So I did. "Fine," I said.

I went back upstairs and changed out of my swim trunks and then I joined Belly in the TV room. I sat as far away from her as I could. The last thing I needed was to catch her cold and be sidelined for a week.

"Why are you still here?" she asked, blowing her nose.

"It's too hot outside," I said. "Wanna watch a movie?"

"It's not that hot outside."

"How would you know if you haven't been out there?"

She narrowed her eyes. "Did your mom make you stay inside with me?"

"No," I said.

"Ha!" Belly grabbed the remote and changed the channel. "I know you're lying."

"I am not!"

Blowing her nose loudly she said, "ESP, remember?"

"That's not real. Can I have the remote?"

She shook her head and held the remote to her chest protectively. "No. My germs are all over it. Sorry. Is there any more toast bread?"

Toast bread was what we called the bread my mom bought at the farmer's market. It came sliced, and it was white and thick and a little bit sweet. I'd had the last three slices of toast bread that morning. I'd slathered it with butter and blackberry jam and I'd eaten it really fast before anyone else got up. With four kids and two adults, bread went really fast. It was every man for himself.

"No more toast bread left," I said.

"Conrad and Steven are such pigs," she said, sniffling.

Guiltily, I said, "I thought all you wanted to eat were grape Popsicles."

She shrugged. "When I woke up this morning I

wanted toast bread. I think maybe I'm getting better."

She didn't look any better to me. Her eyes were swollen and her skin looked grayish, and I don't think she'd washed her hair in days because it was all stringy and matted looking. "Maybe you should take a shower," I said. "My mom says you always feel better after you take a shower."

"Are you saying I smell?"

"Um, no." I looked out the window. It was a clear day, no clouds. I bet Clay was having a blast. I bet Steven and Conrad were too. Conrad had emptied out his old first-grade piggy bank and found a ton of quarters. I bet they'd be at the arcade all afternoon. I wondered how long Clay was gonna be outside. I might be able to catch him in a few hours; it'd still be light out.

I guess Belly caught me staring out the window, because she said, in this really snotty voice, "Just go if you want to."

"I said I didn't," I snapped. Then I took a breath. My mom wouldn't like it if I made Belly upset when she was all sick like this. And she really did look lonely. I kinda felt sorry for her, being stuck inside all day. Summer colds sucked more than anything.

So I said, "Do you want me to teach you how to play poker?"

"You don't know how to play," she scoffed. "Conrad beats you every time."

"Fine," I said. I stood up. I didn't feel *that* sorry for her.

"Never mind," she said. "You can teach me."

I sat back down. "Pass the cards," I said gruffly.

I could tell Belly felt bad because she said, "You shouldn't sit too close. You'll get sick too."

"That's okay," I said. "I never get sick."

"Neither does Conrad," she said, and I rolled my eyes. Belly worshipped Conrad, just like Steven did.

"Conrad does get sick, he gets sick all the time in the winter. He has a weak immune system," I told her, although I didn't know if that was true or not.

She shrugged, but I could tell she didn't believe me. She handed me the cards. "Just deal," she said.

We played poker all afternoon and it was actually pretty fun. I got sick two days later, but I didn't mind that much. Belly stayed home with me and we played more poker and we watched *The Simpsons* a lot.

chapter *thirty-five*
JEREMIAH

As soon as I heard Belly come up the stairs, I met her in the hallway. "So? What's going on?"

"My mom's calling your dad," she said gravely.

"She is? Wow."

"Yeah, so, don't, like, give up already. It's not over yet." Then she gave me one of her wrinkly-nose smiles.

I clapped her on the back and practically sprinted down the stairs. There was Laurel, wiping down the counter. When she saw me, she said, "Your father's coming over. For breakfast."

"Here?"

Laurel nodded. "Will you go to the store and get some things he likes? Eggs and bacon. Muffin mix. And those big grapefruit."

Laurel hated to cook. She had definitely never made

my dad a lumberjack breakfast. "Why are you cooking for him?" I asked.

"Because he's a child and children are cranky when they haven't been fed," she said in that dry way of hers.

Out of nowhere, I said, "Sometimes I hate him."

She hesitated before saying, "Sometimes I do too."

And then I waited for her to say, "But he is your father," the way my mom used to. Laurel didn't, though. Laurel was no bullshit. She didn't say things she didn't mean.

All she said was, "Now get going."

I got up and gave her a bear hug, and she was stiff in my arms. I lifted her up in the air a little, the way I used to do with my mom. "Thanks, Laure," I said. "Really, thanks."

"I'd do anything for you boys. You know that."

"How did you know to come?"

"Belly called me," she said. She narrowed her eyes at me. "Drunk."

Oh, man. "Laure—"

"Don't you 'Laure' me. How could you let her drink? I count on you, Jeremiah. You know that."

Now I felt awful too. The last thing I wanted was for Belly to get in trouble, and I really hated the thought of Laurel thinking badly of me. I'd always tried so hard to look out for Belly, unlike Conrad. If anyone had corrupted her, it was Conrad, not me. Even though I was the one who bought the tequila, not him.

I said, "I'm really sorry. It's just that with my dad's selling the house, and it being our last night, we got carried away. I swear, Laure, it'll never happen again."

She rolled her eyes. "'It'll never happen again'? Don't make promises you can't keep, hon."

"It'll never happen again on my watch," I told her.

Pursing her lips, she said, "We'll see."

I was relieved when she gave me another grimace-smile. "Hurry up and get to the store, will you?"

"Aye aye, sir." I wanted her to smile for real. I knew that if I kept trying, kept joking, she would. She was easy that way.

This time, she really did smile back at me.

chapter *thirty-six*

My mother was right. The shower helped. I tilted my face toward the shower head and let the hot water wash over me and I felt much, much better.

After my shower, I came back downstairs a new woman. My mother was wearing lipstick, and she and Conrad were talking in low voices.

They stopped talking when they saw me standing in the doorway. "Much better," my mother said.

"Where's Jeremiah?" I asked.

"Jeremiah went back to the store. He forgot the grapefruit," she said.

The timer went off and my mother took muffins out of the oven with a dish towel. She accidentally touched the muffin tin with her bare hand and she yelped and dropped the tin on the floor, muffin side down. "Damn!"

Conrad asked if she was okay before I could. "I'm fine," she said, running cold water over her hand.

Then she picked the tin back up and set it on the counter, on top of the towel. I sat down on one of the counter stools and watched my mother empty the muffin tin into a basket. "Our little secret," she said.

The muffins were supposed to cool a little while before you took them out of the tin, but I didn't tell her that. A few were smushed but they mostly looked okay.

"Have a muffin," she said.

I took one, and it was burning hot and falling apart, but it was good. I ate it quickly.

When I was done, my mother said, "You and Conrad take the recycling out."

Without a word, Conrad picked up two of the heavier bags and left me the half-empty one. I followed him outside to the trashcans at the end of the driveway.

"Did you call her?" he asked me.

"I guess I did." I waited for him to call me a baby for calling my mommy the second things got scary.

He didn't. Instead, he said, "Thanks."

I stared at him. "Sometimes you surprise me," I said.

He didn't look at me when he said, "And you hardly ever surprise me. You're still the same."

I glared at him. "Thanks a lot." I dumped my garbage bag in the bin and shut the lid a little too hard.

"No, I mean . . ."

I waited for him to say something, and it seemed like he might have, but then Jeremiah's car came down the street. We both watched Jeremiah park and then bound out of the car with a plastic grocery bag. He strode up to us, his eyes bright. "Hey," he said to me, his bag swinging.

"Hey," I said. I couldn't even look him in the eye. It had all come back to me when I was in the shower. Making Jeremiah dance with me, running away from Conrad, and him picking me up and dropping me in the sand. How humiliating. How awful that they saw me behave that way.

Then Jeremiah gave my hand a squeeze, and when I looked up at him, he said "thank you" so sweetly it hurt.

The three of us walked back to the house. The Police were singing "Message in a Bottle" and the stereo was very loud. Right away my head started pounding and all I wanted was to go back to bed.

"Can we turn down that music?" I asked, rubbing my temples.

"Nope," my mother said, taking the bag from Jeremiah. She pulled out a big grapefruit and tossed it to Conrad. "Squeeze," she said, pointing at the juicer. The juicer was Mr. Fisher's, and it was huge and complicated, one of those Jack LaLanne ones from the late night infomercials.

Conrad snorted. "For him? I'm not squeezing his grapefruit."

"Yes, you will." To me, my mother said, "Mr. Fisher's coming to breakfast."

I squealed. I ran over to her and wrapped my arms around her waist. "It's just breakfast," she warned me. "Don't go getting your hopes up."

But it was too late. I knew she'd change his mind. I knew it. And so did Jeremiah and Conrad. They believed in my mother and so did I—never more so than when Conrad started cutting the grapefruit in half. My mother nodded at him like a drill sergeant. Then she said, "Jere, you set the table, and Belly, you do the eggs."

I started cracking eggs into a bowl, and my mother fried bacon in Susannah's cast iron skillet. She left the bacon grease for me to fry the eggs in. I stirred the eggs around, and the smell of the eggs and the grease made me want to gag. I held my breath as I stirred, and my mother tried to hide a smile as she watched me. "Feeling okay, Belly?" she asked.

I nodded, my teeth clenched.

"Ever planning on drinking again?" she asked conversationally.

I shook my head as hard as I could. "Never, ever again."

When Mr. Fisher arrived half an hour later, we were ready for him. He walked in and looked at the table in amazement. "Wow," he said. "This looks great, Laure. Thank you."

He gave her a meaningful look, the adult co-conspiratorial kind of look.

My mother smiled a Mona Lisa kind of smile. Mr. Fisher wasn't gonna know what hit him. "Let's sit," she said.

We all sat down then. My mother sat next to Mr. Fisher and Jeremiah across from him. I sat next to Conrad. "Dig in," my mother said.

I watched Mr. Fisher pile a mound of eggs on his plate, and then four strips of bacon. He loved bacon, and he really loved it the way my mother made it—incinerated, almost burned to a crisp. I passed on the bacon and eggs and just took a muffin.

My mother poured Mr. Fisher a tall glass of grapefruit juice. "Fresh squeezed, courtesy of your eldest," she said. He took it, a little suspiciously. I couldn't blame him. The only person who had ever squeezed juice for Mr. Fisher was Susannah.

But Mr. Fisher rebounded quickly. He shoveled a forkful of eggs into his mouth and said, "Listen, thanks again for coming to help, Laurel. I really appreciate it." He looked at us kids, smiling. "These guys weren't too keen on listening to what I had to say. I'm glad to have a little backup."

My mother smiled back at him just as pleasantly. "Oh, I'm not here to back you up, Adam. I'm here to back up Beck's boys."

His smile faded. He put down his fork. "Laure—"

"You can't sell this house, Adam. You know that. It

means too much to the kids. It would be a mistake." My mother was calm, matter-of-fact.

Mr. Fisher looked at Conrad and Jeremiah and then back at my mother. "I've already made up my mind, Laurel. Don't make me out to be the bad guy here."

Taking a breath, my mother said, "I'm not making you out to be anything. I'm just trying help you."

Us kids sat absolutely still as we waited for Mr. Fisher to speak. He was struggling to stay calm, but his face was turning red. "I appreciate that. But I've made up my mind. The house is for sale. And frankly, Laurel, you don't get a vote in this. I'm sorry. I know Suze always made you feel like this house was part yours, but it's not."

I almost gasped. My eyes darted back to my mother, and I saw that she, too, was turning red. "Oh, I know that," she said. "This house is pure Beck. It's always been Beck. This was her favorite place. That's why the boys should have it."

Mr. Fisher stood up and pushed out his chair. "I'm not going to argue about this with you, Laurel."

"Adam, sit down," my mother said.

"No, I don't think I will."

My mother's eyes were almost glowing. "I said, sit *down*, Adam." He gaped at her—we all did. Then she said, "Kids, get out."

Conrad opened his mouth to argue but he thought better of it, especially when he saw the look on my mother's face and his dad sit back down. As for me, I couldn't get out of there fast enough. We all hustled out of the kitchen and sat at the top of the stairs, straining to hear.

We didn't have to wait long. Mr. Fisher said, "What the hell, Laurel? Did you really think you could railroad me into changing my mind?"

"Excuse me, but fuck you."

I clapped my hand over my mouth and Conrad's eyes were shining and he was shaking his head in admiration. Jeremiah, though, he looked like he might cry. I reached out and grabbed his hand and gave it a squeeze. When he tried to pull away, I held on tighter.

"This house meant everything to Beck. Can't you get past your own grief and see what it means to the boys? They need this. They *need* this. I don't want to believe that you're this cruel, Adam."

He didn't answer her.

"This house is hers. It's not yours. Don't make me stop you, Adam. Because I will. I'll do everything in my power to keep this house for Beck's boys."

Mr. Fisher said, "What will you do, Laure?" and he sounded so tired.

"I'll do what I have to do."

His voice was muffled when he said, "She's everywhere here. She's everywhere."

He might have been crying. I almost felt sorry for him. I guess my mother did too, because her voice was nearly gentle when she said, "I know. But Adam? You were a sorry excuse for a husband. But she loved you. She really did. She took you back. I tried to talk her out of it, God knows I tried. But she wouldn't listen, because when she sets her mind on someone, that's it. And she set her mind on you, Adam. Earn that. Prove me wrong."

He said something I couldn't quite hear. And then my mother said, "You do this one last thing for her. Okay?"

I looked over at Conrad, and he said in a low voice, to no one in particular, "Laurel is amazing."

I'd never heard anyone describe my mom that way, especially not Conrad. I'd never thought of her as "amazing." But in that moment, she was. She truly was. I said, "Yeah, she is. So was Susannah."

He looked at me for a minute and then he got up and went to his room without waiting to hear what else Mr. Fisher said. He didn't need to. My mother had won. She had done it.

A little while later, when it seemed safe, Jeremiah and I went back downstairs. My mother and Mr. Fisher were drinking coffee the way grown-ups do. His eyes were red-rimmed but hers were the clear eyes of a victor. When he saw us, he said, "Where's Conrad?"

How many times had I heard Mr. Fisher say, "Where's Conrad?" Hundreds. Millions.

"He's upstairs," Jeremiah said.

"Go get him, will you, Jere?"

Jeremiah hesitated and then he looked at my mother, who nodded. He bounded up the stairs and a few minutes later, Conrad was with him. Conrad's face was guarded, cautious.

"I'll make you a deal," Mr. Fisher said. This was the old Mr. Fisher, power broker, negotiator. He loved to make deals. He used to offer trades to us kids. Like, he'd drive us to the go-kart track if we swept the sand out of the garage. Or he'd take the boys fishing if they cleaned out all the tackle boxes.

Warily, Conrad said, "What do you want? My trust fund?"

Mr. Fisher's jaw tightened. "No. I want you back at school tomorrow. I want you to finish your exams. If you do that, the house is yours. Yours and Jeremiah's."

Jeremiah whooped loudly. "Yes!" he shouted. He reached over and enveloped Mr. Fisher in a guy hug, and Mr. Fisher clapped him on the back.

"What's the catch?" Conrad asked.

"No catch. But you have to make at least Cs. No Ds or Fs." Mr. Fisher had always prided himself on driving the hard bargain. "Do we have a deal?"

Conrad hesitated. I knew right away what was wrong. Conrad didn't want to owe his dad anything. Even though this was what he wanted, even though it was why he had come here. He didn't want to take anything from his dad.

"I haven't studied," he said. "I might not pass."

He was testing him. Conrad had never "not passed." He'd never gotten anything below a B, and even Bs were rare.

"Then no deal," Mr. Fisher said. "Those are the terms."

Urgently, Jeremiah said, "Con, just say yes, man. We'll help you study. Won't we, Belly?"

Conrad looked at me, and I looked at my mother. "Can I, Mom?"

My mother nodded. "You can stay, but you have to be home tomorrow."

"Take the deal," I told Conrad.

"All right," he said at last.

"Shake on it like a man, then," Mr. Fisher said, holding out his hand.

Reluctantly, Conrad extended his arm and they shook. My mother caught my eye and she mouthed, *Shake on it like a man*, and I knew she was thinking how sexist Mr. Fisher was. But it didn't matter. We had won.

"Thanks, Dad," Jeremiah said. "Really, thanks."

He hugged his dad again and Mr. Fisher hugged him back, saying, "I need to get back to the city." Then he nodded at me. "Thanks for helping Conrad, Belly."

I said, "You're welcome." But I didn't know what I was saying "you're welcome" for, because I hadn't really done anything. My mother had helped Conrad more in half an hour than I had in all my time of knowing him.

After Mr. Fisher left, my mother got up and started rinsing dishes. I joined her and loaded them into the dishwasher. I rested my head on her shoulder for a second. I said, "Thank you."

"You're welcome."

"You were a real badass, Mom."

"Don't cuss," she said, the corners of her mouth turning up.

"You're one to talk."

Then we washed the dishes in silence, and my mother had that sad look on her face and I knew she was thinking of Susannah. And I wished there was something I could say to take that look away, but sometimes there just weren't words.

The three of us walked her to the car. "You boys will get her home tomorrow?" she asked, throwing her bag onto the passenger seat.

"Definitely," Jeremiah said.

Then Conrad said, "Laurel." He hesitated. "You're coming back, aren't you?"

My mother turned to him, surprised. She was touched. "You want an old lady like me around?" she asked. "Sure, I'll be back whenever you'll have me."

"When?" he asked. He looked so young, so vulnerable my heart ached a little.

I guessed my mother was feeling the same way, because

she reached out and touched his cheek. My mother was not a cheek-touching kind of person. It just wasn't her way. But it was Susannah's. "Before the summer's over, and I'll come back to close the house up too."

My mother got into the car then. She waved at us as she backed down the driveway, her sunglasses on, the window down. "See you soon," she called out.

Jeremiah waved and Conrad said, "See you soon."

My mother told me once that when Conrad was very young, he called her "his Laura." "Where is my Laura?" he'd say, wandering around looking for her. She said he followed her everywhere; he'd even follow her into the bathroom. He called her his girlfriend and he would bring her sand crabs and seashells from the ocean and he would lay them at her feet. When she told me about it, I thought, *What I wouldn't give to have Conrad Fisher call me his girlfriend and bring me shells.*

"I'm sure he doesn't remember," she'd said, smiling faintly.

"Why don't you ask him if he does?" I'd said. I loved hearing stories about when Conrad was little. I loved to tease him, because the opportunity to tease Conrad came up so rarely.

She'd said, "No, that would embarrass him," and I'd said, "So what? Isn't that the point?"

And she'd said, "Conrad is sensitive. He has a lot of pride. Let him have that."

The way she said that, I could tell that she really got him. Understood him in a way that I didn't. I was jealous of that, of both of them.

"What was I like?" I'd asked.

"You? You were my baby."

"But what was I *like*?" I persisted.

"You used to chase after the boys. It was so cute the way you'd follow them around, trying to impress them." My mother laughed. "They used to get you to dance around and do tricks."

"Like a puppy?" I frowned at the thought.

She'd waved me off. "Oh, you were fine. You just liked to be included."

chapter *thirty-seven*
JEREMIAH

The day Laurel came, the house was a wreck and I was in my boxers ironing my white button-down. I was already late for senior banquet and I was in a foul mood. My mom had barely said two words all day and even Nona couldn't get her to talk.

I was supposed to pick up Mara, and she hated it when I was late. She'd get all pissy and she'd sit and sulk for about as long as I'd made her wait.

I had put down the iron for a second so I could turn the shirt over and I ended up burning the back of my arm. "Shit!" I yelled. It really freaking hurt.

That was when Laurel showed up. She walked through the front door and saw me standing in the living room in my boxers, holding the back of my arm.

"Run some cold water over it," she told me. I ran to

the kitchen and held my arm under the faucet for a few minutes, and when I came back, she had finished the shirt and gotten started on my khakis.

"Do you wear yours with a crease down the front?" she asked me.

"Uh, sure," I said. "What are you doing here, Laurel? It's a Tuesday." Laurel usually came on weekends and stayed in the guest room.

"I just came to check on things," she said, running the iron down the front of the pants. "I had a free afternoon."

"My mom's asleep already," I told her. "With the new medicine she's taking, she sleeps all the time."

"That's good," Laurel said. "And what about you? Why are you getting all dressed up?"

I sat down on the couch and put my socks on. "I've got senior banquet tonight," I told her.

Laurel handed me my shirt and pants. "What time does it start?"

I glanced at the grandfather clock in the foyer. "Ten minutes ago," I said, stepping into my pants.

"You'd better get going."

"Thanks for ironing my clothes," I said.

I was grabbing my keys when I heard my mom call my name from her bedroom. I turned toward her doorway, and Laurel said, "Just go to your banquet, Jere. I've got it covered."

I hesitated. "Are you sure?"

"A thousand percent. Beat it."

I sped all the way to Mara's house. She came out as soon as I pulled into her driveway. She was wearing that red dress I liked and she looked nice, and I was about to tell her so, but then she said, "You're late."

I shut my mouth. Mara didn't speak to me for the rest of the night, not even when we won Cutest Couple. She didn't feel like going to Patan's party afterward and neither did I. The whole time we were out, I was thinking about my mom and feeling guilty for being gone so long.

When we got to Mara's house, she didn't get out right away, which was her signal that she wanted to talk. I shut off the engine.

"So, what's up? Are you still mad at me for being late, Mar?"

She looked pained. "I just want to know if we're going to stay together. Can you just tell me what you want to do, and then we'll do it?"

"Honestly, I can't really think about this kind of stuff right now."

"I know. I'm sorry."

"But if I was going to have to say whether or not I think we'll be together when we're at school in the fall, long distance—" I hesitated, and then I just said it. "I would probably say no."

Mara started crying, and I felt like a real piece of shit. I should've just lied.

"That's what I thought," she said. Then she kissed me on the cheek and ran out of the car and into her house.

So that's how we broke up. If I'm going to be completely honest, I'll admit that it was a relief not to have to think about Mara anymore. The only person I had room in my head for was my mom.

When I got home, my mom and Laurel were still up playing cards and listening to music. For the first time in days, I heard my mom laugh.

Laurel didn't leave the next day. She stayed all week. At the time, I didn't wonder about her job, or all the other stuff she had going on at home. I was just grateful to have an adult around.

chapter *thirty-eight*

The three of us walked back to the house. The sun was hot on my back and I thought about how nice it would be to lay out on the beach for a while, to sleep the afternoon away and wake up tan. But there wasn't any time for that, not when we needed to get Conrad ready for his midterms by tomorrow.

When we got inside, Conrad fell onto the couch and Jeremiah sprawled out on the floor. "So tired," he moaned.

What my mother did for us, for me, was a gift. Now it was my turn to give one back. "Get up," I said.

Neither of them moved. Conrad's eyes were closed. So I threw a pillow at Conrad and jabbed Jeremiah in the stomach with my foot. "We have to start studying, you lazy bums. Now get up!"

Conrad opened his eyes. "I'm too tired to study. I need to take a power nap first."

"Me too," Jeremiah said.

Crossing my arms, I glared at them and said, "I'm tired too, you know. But look at the clock; it's already one. We're gonna have to work all night and leave really early tomorrow morning."

Shrugging, Conrad said, "I work best under pressure."

"But—"

"Seriously, Belly. I can't work like this. Just let me sleep for an hour."

Jeremiah was already falling asleep. I sighed. I couldn't fight the both of them. "Fine. One hour. But that's it."

I stalked into the kitchen and poured myself a Coke. I was tempted to take a nap too, but that would be setting the wrong example.

While they slept, I kicked the plan into gear. I got Conrad's books out of the car, brought his laptop downstairs, and set up the kitchen like a study room. I plugged in lamps, stacked books and binders according to subject, put out pens and paper. Last, I brewed a big pot of coffee, and even though I didn't drink coffee, I knew mine was good, because I brewed a pot for my mother every morning. Then I took Jeremiah's car and drove to McDonald's to pick up cheeseburgers. They loved McDonald's cheeseburgers. They used to have cheeseburger-eating contests and they'd stack them up like pancakes. Sometimes they let me play too. One time, I won. I ate nine cheeseburgers.

I let them sleep an extra half hour—but only because it took me that long to get things set up. Then I filled up Susannah's spray bottle, the one she'd used to water her more delicate plants. I sprayed Conrad first, right in the eyes.

"Hey," he said, waking up right away. He wiped his face with the bottom of his T-shirt, and I gave him another spray just because.

"Rise and shine," I sang.

Then I walked over to Jeremiah and sprayed him, too. He didn't wake up though. He had always been impossible to wake up. He could sleep through a tidal wave. I sprayed and sprayed and when he just rolled over, I unscrewed the top of the bottle and poured the water right down the back of his T-shirt.

He finally woke up and stretched his arms out, still lying down on the floor. He gave me a slow grin, like he was used to being woken up this way. "Morning," he said. Jeremiah might have been hard to wake up, but he was never a grouch when he finally did.

"It's not morning. It's almost three o'clock in the afternoon. I let you guys sleep an extra half an hour so you better be grateful," I snapped.

"I am," Jeremiah said, reaching his arm out for me to help him up. I grudgingly gave him my hand and helped heft him up. "Come on," I said.

They followed me into the kitchen.

"What the—," Conrad said, looking around the room at all his things.

Jeremiah clapped his hands together and then he held one hand up for a high five, which I gave him. "You're amazing," he said. Then he sniffed and spotted the greasy white McDonald's bag and lit up. "Yes! Mickey D's cheeseburgers! I'd know that smell anywhere."

I smacked his hand away. "Not yet. There is a reward system in place here. Conrad studies, and then he gets food."

Jeremiah frowned. "What about me?"

"Conrad studies, and you get food."

Conrad raised his eyebrows at me. "A reward system, huh? What else do I get?"

I flushed. "Just the cheeseburgers."

His eyes flickered over me appraisingly, like he was trying to decide whether or not he wanted to buy a coat. I could feel my cheeks heat up as he looked at me. "As much as I like the sound of a reward system, I'm gonna pass," he said at last.

"What are you talking about?" Jeremiah asked.

Conrad shrugged. "I study better on my own. I've got it covered. You guys can go."

Jeremiah shook his head in disgust. "Just like always. You can't handle asking for help. Well, sucks to be you, 'cause we're staying."

"What do you guys know about freshman psych?" Conrad said, crossing his arms.

Jeremiah sprang up. "We'll figure it out." He winked at me. "Bells, can we eat first? I need grease."

I felt like I had won a prize. Like I was invincible. Reaching into the bag, I said, "One each. That's it."

When Conrad's back was turned, as he was rummaging around the cupboard for Tabasco sauce, Jeremiah held his hand out for another high five. I slapped it silently and we grinned at each other. Jeremiah and I were a good team, always had been.

We ate our cheeseburgers in silence. As soon as we were done, I said, "How do you want to do this, Conrad?"

"Seeing as how I don't want to do this at all, I'll let you decide," he said. He had mustard on his lower lip.

"Okay, then." I was prepared for this. "You'll read. I'll work on note cards for psych. Jeremiah will highlight."

"Jere doesn't know how to highlight," Conrad scoffed.

"Hey!" Jeremiah said. Then, turning to me, he said, "He's right. I suck at highlighting. I just end up highlighting the whole page. I'll do note cards and you highlight, Bells."

I ripped open a pack of index cards and handed them to Jeremiah. Incredibly enough, Conrad listened. He picked his psych textbook out of the stack of books and he started to read.

Sitting at the table, studying with his forehead creased,

he looked like the old Conrad. The one who cared about things like exams and ironed shirts and being on time. The irony of all this was that Jeremiah had never been much of a student. He hated to study; he hated grades. Learning was, had always been, Conrad's thing. From the very start, he was the one with the chemistry set, thinking up experiments for us to do as his scientist's assistants. I remembered when he'd discovered the word "absurd," and he went around saying it all the time. "That's *absurd*," he'd say. Or "numbskull," his favorite insult—he said that a lot too. The summer he was ten, he tried to work his way through the *Encyclopedia Britannica*. When we came back the next summer, he was at *Q*.

I realized it suddenly. I missed him. All this time. When you got to the underneath of it, there it was. There it had always been. And even though he was sitting there only feet away, I missed him more than ever.

Underneath my lashes I watched him, and I thought, *Come back. Be the you I love and remember.*

chapter *thirty-nine*

We were done with psychology and Conrad was working on his English paper with his headphones on when my phone buzzed. It was Taylor. I wasn't sure if she was calling to apologize or to demand I bring her stuff back home immediately. Maybe a mixture of both. I turned off my phone.

With all the house drama, I hadn't thought about our fight once. I'd only been back at the summer house for a couple of days, and just like always, I'd already forgotten about Taylor and everything back home. What mattered to me was here. It had always been that way.

But those things she'd said, they hurt. Maybe they were true. But I didn't know if I could forgive her for saying them.

It was getting dark out when Jeremiah leaned over

and said in a low voice, "You know, if you wanted to, you could leave tonight. You could just take my car. I could pick it up tomorrow, after Conrad's done with his exams. We could hang out or something."

"Oh, I'm not leaving yet. I want to go with you guys tomorrow."

"Are you sure?"

"Sure, I'm sure. Don't you want me to come with you?" It was starting to hurt my feelings, the way he was acting like they were imposing on me, as if we weren't family.

"Yeah, course I do." He paused like he was going to say something else.

I poked him with my highlighter. "Are you scared that you'll get in trouble with *Mara*?" I was only halfway teasing. I still couldn't believe he hadn't told me he had a sort of girlfriend. I wasn't entirely sure why it mattered, but it did. We were supposed to be close. Or at least we used to be. I should have known if he had a girlfriend or not. And how long had they been "broken up" anyway? She hadn't been at the funeral, or at least I didn't think so. It wasn't like Jeremiah had gone around introducing her to people. What kind of girlfriend didn't go to her boyfriend's mom's funeral? Even Conrad's ex had come.

Jeremiah glanced over at Conrad and lowered his voice. "I told you, Mara and I are done."

When I didn't say anything, he said, "Come on, Belly. Don't be mad."

"I can't believe you didn't tell me about her," I said, highlighting an entire paragraph. I didn't look at him. "I can't believe you kept it a secret."

"There wasn't anything to tell, I swear."

"Ha!" I said. But I felt better. I snuck a peek at Jeremiah, and he looked back at me with anxious eyes.

"Okay?"

"Fine. It doesn't affect me one way or the other. I just thought you would have told me a thing like that."

He relaxed back into his seat. "We weren't that serious, trust me. She was just a girl. It wasn't like how it was with Conrad and—"

I started, and he broke off guiltily.

It wasn't like how it was with Conrad and Aubrey. He'd loved her. Once upon a time, he'd been crazy about her. He had never been that way with me. Never. But I had loved him. I loved him longer and truer than I had anyone in my whole life and I would probably never love anyone that way again. Which, to be honest, was almost a relief.

chapter *forty*

JULY 6

When I woke up the next morning, the first thing I did was go to my window. Who knew how many more times I would see this view? We were all growing up. I would be at college soon. But the good thing, the comforting thing, was the knowing that it would still be here. The house wasn't going away.

Looking out the window, it was impossible to see where the sky ended and the ocean began. I'd forgotten how foggy the mornings could get here. I stood there and tried to get my fill, tried to make the memory last.

Then I ran over to Jeremiah's and Conrad's rooms, banging on doors. "Wake up! Let's get this show on the road!" I yelled, starting down the hall.

I headed downstairs to get a glass of juice, and Conrad was sitting at the kitchen table, where he'd been when I went to sleep around four a.m. He was already dressed and making notes in a notebook.

I started to back out of the kitchen, but he looked up. "Nice pjs," he said.

I flushed. I was still wearing Taylor's stupid pajamas. Scowling, I said, "We're leaving in twenty minutes, so be ready."

As I headed back upstairs, I heard Conrad say, "I already am."

If he said he was ready, he was ready. He would pass those exams. He'd probably ace them. Conrad didn't fail at anything he set his mind to.

An hour later, we were almost on our way. I was locking the glass sliding door on the porch when I heard Conrad say, "Should we?"

I turned around, started to say, "Should we what?" when Jeremiah came out of nowhere.

"Yeah. For old times' sake," Jeremiah said.

Uh-oh. "No way," I said. "No freaking way."

The next thing I knew, Jeremiah was grabbing my legs and Conrad took my arms, and together they swung me back, then forth. Jeremiah yelled, "Belly Flop!" and they flung me through the air, and as I landed in the pool, I thought, *Well, there, they're finally united on something*.

When I surfaced, I yelled, "Jerks!" It only made them laugh harder.

I had to go back inside and change out of my soaked clothes, the clothes I wore the first day. I changed into Taylor's sundress and her platform sandals. As I wrung out my hair with a hand towel, it was hard to be mad. I even smiled to myself. Possibly the last Belly Flop of my life, and Steven wasn't there to partake.

It was Jeremiah's idea to take one car, so Conrad could keep studying on the way. Conrad didn't even try to take the front seat, he just went straight to the back and started flipping through his note cards.

Predictably, I cried as we drove away. I was just glad I was up front and wearing sunglasses so the boys couldn't tease me about it. But I loved that house, and I hated to say good-bye. Because, it was more than just a house. It was every summer, every boat ride, every sunset. It was Susannah.

We drove in near silence for a while, and then Britney Spears came on the radio, and I turned it up, loud. It went without saying that Conrad hated Britney Spears, but I didn't care. I started to sing along, and Jeremiah did too.

"Oh baby baby, I shouldn't have let you go," I sang, shimmying toward the dashboard.

"Show me how you want it to be," Jeremiah sang back, bouncing his shoulders.

When the song changed, it was Justin Timberlake, and Jeremiah did an amazing Justin Timberlake. He was so un-self-conscious and easy with who he was. He made me want to be like that too.

He sang to me, "And tell me how they got that pretty little face on that pretty little frame, girl." I put my hand on my heart and fake-swooned for him, like a groupie.

"Fast fast slow, whichever way you wanna run, girl."

I backed him up at the chorus. "This just can't be summer love . . ."

From the backseat, Conrad growled, "Can you guys please turn the music down? I'm trying to study here, remember?"

I turned around and said, "Oh, sorry. Is it bothering you?"

He looked at me with narrowed eyes.

Without saying a word, Jeremiah turned the music down. We drove for another hour or so and then he said, "Do you need to pee or anything? I'm gonna stop at the next exit for gas."

I shook my head. "No, but I am thirsty."

We pulled into the gas station parking lot, and while Jeremiah filled the car up and Conrad napped, I ran into the convenience store. I got Jeremiah and me both Slurpees, half Coke and half cherry, a combination I had perfected over the years.

When I got back to the car, I climbed in and handed Jeremiah his Slurpee. His whole face lit up. "Aw, thanks, Bells. What flavor did you get me?"

"Drink it and see."

He took a long sip and nodded appreciatively. "Half Coke, half cherry, your specialty. Nice."

"Hey, remember that time—," I started to say.

"Yup," he said. "My dad still doesn't want anyone touching his blender."

I put my feet up on the dashboard and leaned back, sipping on my Slurpee. I thought to myself, *Happiness is a Slurpee and a hot pink straw.*

From the back, Conrad said, irritably, "Where's mine?"

"I thought you were still asleep," I said. "And you have to drink a Slurpee right away or it'll melt, so . . . I didn't see the point."

Conrad glared at me. "Well, at least let me have a sip."

"But you hate Slurpees." Which was true. Conrad didn't like sugary drinks, he never had.

"I don't care. I'm thirsty."

I handed him my cup and turned around and watched him drink. I was expecting him to make a face or something, but he just drank and handed it back. And then he said, "I thought your specialty was cocoa."

I stared at him. Did he really just say that? Did he remember? The way he looked back at me, one eyebrow raised, I knew he did. And this time, I was the one to look away.

Because I remembered. I remembered everything.

chapter *forty-one*

When Conrad left to take his exam, Jeremiah and I bought turkey and avocado sandwiches on whole wheat bread and we ate them out on the lawn. I finished mine first; I was really hungry.

When he was done, Jeremiah balled up the foil in his hand and threw it into the trashcan. He sat back down next to me in the grass. Out of nowhere, he said to me, "Why didn't you come see me after my mom died?"

I stuttered, "I d-d-did, I came to the funeral."

Jeremiah's gaze on me was steady, unblinking. "That's not what I mean."

"I—I didn't think you'd want me there yet."

"No, it was because *you* didn't want to be there. I wanted you there."

He was right. I didn't want to be there. I didn't want to

be anywhere near her house. Thinking about her made my heart hurt; it was too much. But the thought of Jeremiah waiting for me to call him, needing someone to talk to, that hurt so bad. "You're right," I told him. "I should've come."

Jeremiah had been there for Conrad, for Susannah. For me. And who had been there for him? Nobody. I wanted him to know I was here now.

He looked up at the sky. "It's hard, you know? Because I want to talk about her. But Conrad doesn't want to, and I can't talk to my dad, and you weren't there either. We all love her, and nobody can talk about her."

"What do you want to say?"

He leaned his head back, thinking. "That I miss her. I really miss her. She's only been gone for two months, but it feels like longer. And it also feels like it just happened, like yesterday."

I nodded. That was exactly how it felt.

"Do you think she'd be glad?"

He meant glad about Conrad, the way we'd helped him. "Yeah."

"Me too." Jeremiah hesitated. "So what now?"

"What do you mean?"

"I mean, are you going to come back this summer?"

"Well, sure. When my mom comes, I'll come too."

He nodded. "Good. Because my dad was wrong, you know. It's your house too. And Laure's, and Steve's. It's all of ours."

Suddenly I was struck with the strangest sensation, of wanting, needing, to reach out and touch his cheek with the back of my hand. So he would know, so he would *feel* exactly how much those words meant to me. Because sometimes words were so pitifully inadequate, and I knew that, but I had to try anyway. I told him, "Thank you. That means—a lot."

He shrugged. "It's just the truth."

We saw him coming from far away, walking fast. We stood up and waited for him.

Jeremiah said, "Does it look like good news to you? It looks like good news to me."

It did to me, too.

Conrad strode up to us, his eyes gleaming. "I killed it," he said triumphantly. First time I'd seen him smile, really smile—joyful, carefree—since Susannah died. He and Jeremiah high-fived so hard the clap rang out in the air. And then Conrad smiled at me, and whirled me around so fast I almost tripped.

I was laughing. "See? See? I told you!"

Conrad picked me up and threw me over his shoulder like I weighed nothing, just like he had the other night. I laughed as he ran, weaving left and right like he was on a football field. "Put me down!" I shrieked, yanking at the bottom of my dress.

He did. He set me down on the ground gently. "Thanks," he said, his hand still on my waist. "For coming."

Before I could tell him you're welcome, Jeremiah walked over and said, "You still have one left, Con." His voice was strained, and I straightened my dress.

Conrad looked at his watch. "You're right. I'm gonna head over to the psychology department. This will be a quick one. I'll meet up with you guys in an hour or so."

As I watched him go, a million questions ran through my head. I felt dizzy, and not just from being spun around in the air.

Abruptly, Jeremiah said, "I'm gonna go find a bathroom. I'll meet you at the car." He fished his keys out of his pocket and threw them to me.

"Do you want me to wait?" I asked, but he was already walking away.

He didn't turn around. "No, just go ahead."

Instead of going straight to the car, I stopped at the student store. I bought a soda and a hoodie that said BROWN in block letters. Even though it wasn't cold, I put it on.

Jeremiah and I sat in the car, listening to the radio. It was starting to get dark. The windows were down and I could hear a bird calling somewhere out there. Conrad would be done with his last exam soon.

"Nice hoodie, by the way," Jeremiah said.

"Thanks. I always wanted one from Brown."

Jeremiah nodded. "I remember."

I fingered my necklace, twisting it around my pinky.

"I wonder . . ." I let my sentence trail off, waiting for Jeremiah to prod me, to ask me what it was I wondered about. But he didn't. He didn't ask me anything.

He was silent.

Sighing, I looked out the window and asked, "Does he ever talk about me? I mean, has he ever said anything?"

"Don't," he snapped.

"Don't what?" I turned toward him, confused.

"Don't ask me that. Don't ask me about him." Jeremiah spoke in a harsh, low voice, a tone he'd never used with me and one I didn't recall him using with anybody. A muscle in his jaw twitched furiously.

I recoiled and sank back into my seat. I felt as though he had slapped me. "What's the matter with you?"

He started to say something, maybe an apology and maybe not, and then he stopped, he leaned over and pulled me toward him—like by gravitational force. He kissed me, hard, and his skin was stubbly and rough against my cheek. My first thought was, *I guess he didn't have time to shave this morning*, and then—I was kissing him back, my fingers winding through his soft yellow hair and my eyes closed. He kissed like he was drowning and I was air. It was passionate, and desperate, and like nothing I had ever experienced before.

This was what people meant when they said the earth stopped turning. It felt like a world outside of that car, that moment, didn't exist. It was just us.

When he backed away, his pupils were huge and unfocused. He blinked, and then he cleared his throat. "Belly," he said, and his voice was foggy. He didn't say anything else, just my name.

"Do you still—" Care. Think about me. Want me.

Roughly, he said, "Yes. Yes, I still."

And then we were kissing again.

He must have made some noise, because we both looked up at the same time.

We sprang apart. There was Conrad, looking right at us. He had stopped short of the car. His face was white.

He said, "No, don't stop. I'm the one who's interrupting."

He turned jerkily and started off. Jeremiah and I stared at each other in silent horror. And then my hand was on the door handle and I was on my feet. I didn't look back.

I ran after him and called his name, but Conrad didn't turn around. I grabbed his arm and he finally looked at me, and there was so much hate in his eyes I winced. Even though, on some level, wasn't this what I wanted? To make his heart hurt the way he made mine? Or maybe, to make him feel something for me other than pity or indifference. To make him feel something, anything.

"So you like Jeremiah now?" He meant to sound sarcastic, cruel, and he did, but he also sounded pained. Like he cared about the answer.

Which made me feel glad. And sad.

I said, "I don't know. Does it matter to you if I do?"

He stared at me, and then he leaned forward and touched the necklace around my neck. The one I'd been hiding under my shirt all day.

"If you like Jeremiah, why are you wearing my necklace?"

I wet my lips. "I found it when we were packing up your dorm room. It doesn't mean anything."

"You know what it means."

I shook my head. "I don't." But of course I did. I remembered when he'd explained the concept of infinity to me. Immeasurable, one moment stretching out to the next. He bought me that necklace. He knew what it meant.

"Then give it back." He held his hand out, and I saw that it was shaking.

"No," I said.

"It's not yours. I never gave it to you. You just took it."

That's when I finally got it. I finally understood. It wasn't the thought that counted. It was the actual execution that mattered, the showing up for somebody. The intent behind it wasn't enough. Not for me. Not anymore. It wasn't enough to know that deep down, he loved me. You had to actually say it to somebody, show them that you cared. And he just didn't. Not enough.

I could feel him waiting for me to argue, to protest,

to plead. But I didn't do any of those things. I struggled for what felt like eternity, trying to undo the clasp on the necklace around my neck. Which was no surprise, considering the fact that my hands were shaking too. I finally got the chain free and I handed it back to him.

Surprise registered upon his face for the tiniest of moments, and then, like always, he was closed off again. Maybe I'd imagined it. That he'd cared.

He stuffed the necklace into his pocket. "Then leave," he said.

When I didn't move, he said, sharply, "Go!"

I was a tree, rooted to the spot. My feet were frozen.

"Go to Jeremiah. He's the one who wants you," Conrad said. "I don't. I never did."

And then I was stumbling, running away.

chapter *forty-two*

I didn't go back to the car right away. All I had in front of me were impossible choices. How could I face Jeremiah after what just happened? After we kissed, after I went running after Conrad? My mind was spinning in a million different directions. I kept touching my lips. Then I'd touch my collarbone, where the necklace used to be. I wandered around campus, but after a while, I headed back to the car. What choice did I have? I couldn't just leave without telling anybody. And it wasn't like I had another way home.

I guessed Conrad was thinking the same thing, because when I got back to the car, he was already there, sitting in the backseat with the window open. Jeremiah was sitting on the hood of the car. "Hi," he said.

"Hey." I hesitated, unsure of what was next. For once,

our ESP connection failed me, because I had no idea what he was thinking. His face was unreadable.

He slid off the car. "Ready to go home?"

I nodded, and he threw me the keys. "You drive," he said.

In the car, Conrad ignored me completely. I didn't exist to him anymore, and despite everything I'd said, that made me want to die. I never should have come. None of us were speaking to one another. I'd lost them both.

What would Susannah say if she saw the mess we were in now? She would have been so disappointed in me. I hadn't been a help at all. I'd only made things worse.

Just when we thought everything was going to be okay, we all fell apart.

I'd been driving for what felt like forever when it started to rain. It started out with fat little *plops* and then it came down heavy, in hard sheets.

"Can you see?" Jeremiah asked me.

"Yeah," I lied. I could barely see two feet in front of me. The windshield wipers were swishing back and forth furiously.

Traffic had been crawling along, and then it slowed almost to a stop. There were police lights way up ahead.

"There must have been an accident," Jeremiah said.

We'd been sitting in traffic for over an hour when it started to hail.

I looked at Conrad in the rearview, but his face was

impassive. He might as well have been somewhere else. "Should we pull over?"

"Yeah. Get off at the next exit and see if we can find a gas station," Jeremiah said, glancing at the clock. It was ten thirty.

The rain didn't let up. We sat in the gas station parking lot for what felt like forever. The rain was loud, but we were so quiet that when my stomach growled, I was pretty sure they both heard. I coughed to cover up the noise.

Jeremiah jumped out of the car and ran inside the gas station. When he ran back, his hair was dripping wet and matted. He tossed me a packet of peanut butter and cheese crackers without looking at me. "There's a motel a few miles down," he said, wiping his forehead with the back of his arm.

"Let's just wait it out," Conrad said. It was the first time he'd spoken since we'd left.

"Dude, the highway's pretty much shut down. There's no point. I say we just crash for a few hours and leave in the morning."

Conrad didn't say anything.

I didn't say anything because I was too busy eating the crackers. They were bright orange and salty and gritty, and I stuffed them into my mouth, one after the other. I didn't even offer one to either of them.

"Belly, what do you want to do?" Jeremiah said it very

politely, like I was his cousin from out of town. Like his mouth hadn't been on mine just hours before.

I swallowed my last cracker. "I don't care. Do whatever you want."

By the time we got to the motel, it was midnight.

I went to the bathroom to call my mother. I told her what had happened and right away she said, "I'm coming to get you."

Every part of me wanted to say *Yes, please, come right this second*, but she sounded so tired, and she'd already done so much. So instead I said, "No, it's fine, Mom."

"It's all right, Belly. It's not that far."

"It's okay, really. We'll leave early tomorrow morning."

She yawned. "Is the motel in a safe area?"

"Yes." Even though I didn't know exactly where we were or if it constituted a safe area. But it seemed safe enough.

"Just go to sleep and get up first thing. Call me when you're on the road."

After we got off the phone I leaned against the wall for a minute. How did I end up here?

I changed into Taylor's pajamas and put my new hoodie on over them.

I took my time brushing my teeth and taking out my contact lenses. I didn't care that the boys might be waiting to use the bathroom. I just wanted time alone, away from them. When I came back out, Jeremiah and Conrad were on the floor, on opposite sides of the bed. They each had a pillow and a blanket. "You guys should take the bed," I said, even though I only partly meant it. "There's two of you. I'll sleep on the floor."

Conrad was busy ignoring me, but Jeremiah said, "Nah, you take it. You're the girl."

Under ordinary circumstances, I would have argued with him just for the principle of it—what did my being a girl have to do with whether or not I slept on the floor? I was a girl, not an invalid. But I didn't argue. I was too tired. And I did want the bed.

I crawled onto the bed and got under the covers. Jeremiah set the alarm on his phone and shut off the lights. Nobody said good night or suggested we see if there was anything good on TV.

I tried to fall asleep but I couldn't. I tried to remember the last time the three of us had slept in the same room. I couldn't at first, but then I did.

We'd pitched a tent on the beach and I'd begged and begged to be included and finally my mother made them let me come. Me and Steven and Jeremiah and Conrad. We played Uno for hours and Steven high-fived me when I won twice in a row. Suddenly I missed my big brother so much I wanted to cry. Part of me thought that if Steven had been there, things wouldn't have gotten this awful. Maybe none of this would have happened, because I would still be chasing after the boys instead of being in the middle.

But now everything had changed and we could never go back to the way things used to be.

I was lying in bed thinking about all of this when I heard Jeremiah snoring, which really annoyed me. He'd always been able to fall asleep at will, as soon as his head hit the pillow. I guessed he wasn't losing any sleep over what had happened. I guessed I shouldn't either. I flipped over on my other side, facing away from Jeremiah.

And then I heard Conrad say, quietly, "Earlier, when I said I never wanted you. I didn't mean it."

My breath caught. I didn't know what to say or if I was even supposed to say anything. All I knew was, this was what I'd been waiting for. This exact moment. Exactly this.

I opened my mouth to speak, and then he said it again. "I didn't mean it."

I held my breath, waiting to hear what he'd say next.

All he said was, "Good night, Belly."

After that, of course I couldn't sleep. My head was too full of things to think about. What did he mean? That he wanted to be, like, together? Me and him, for real? It was what I'd wanted my whole life, but then there was Jeremiah's face in the car, open and wanting and needing me. In that moment, I'd wanted and needed him, too, more than I had ever known. Had it always been there? But after tonight, I didn't even know if he wanted me anymore. Maybe it was too late.

Then there was Conrad. *I didn't mean it.* I closed my eyes and heard him say those words again and again. His voice, traveling across the dark, it haunted me and it thrilled me.

So I lay there barely breathing, going over every word. The boys were asleep and every part of me was fully awake and alive. It was like a really amazing dream, and I was afraid to fall asleep because when I woke up, it would be gone.

chapter *forty-three*
JULY 7

I woke up before Jeremiah's alarm went off. I took a shower, brushed my teeth, put on the same clothes as the day before.

When I came out, Jeremiah was on the phone and Conrad was folding up his blanket. I waited for him to look at me. If he would just look at me, smile, say something, I would know what to do.

But Conrad didn't look up. He put the blankets back in the closet and then he put on his sneakers. He undid the laces and pulled them tighter. I kept waiting, but he wouldn't look at me.

"Hey," I said.

He finally raised his head. "Hey," he said. "A friend of mine is coming to get me."

"Why?" I asked.

"It's easier this way. He'll take me back to Cousins so

I can get my car, and J can take you home."

"Oh," I said. I was so surprised, it took a moment for the disappointment, the utter disbelief, to register.

We stood there, looking at each other, saying nothing. But it was the kind of nothing that meant everything. In his eyes, there was no trace of what had happened between us earlier, and I could feel something inside me break.

So that was that. We were finally, finally over.

I looked at him, and I felt so sad, because this thought occurred to me: *I will never look at you in the same way ever again. I'll never be that girl again. The girl who comes running back every time you push her away, the girl who loves you anyway.*

I couldn't even be mad at him, because this was who he was. This was who he'd always been. He'd never lied about that. He gave and then he took away. I felt it in the pit of my stomach, the familiar ache, that lost, regretful feeling only he could give me. I never wanted to feel it again. Never, ever.

Maybe this was why I came, so I could really know. So I could say good-bye.

I looked at him, and I thought, *If I was very brave or very honest, I would tell him.* I would say it, so he would know it and I would know it, and I could never take it back. But I wasn't that brave or honest, so all I did was look at him. And I think he knew anyway.

I release you. I evict you from my heart. Because if I don't do it now, I never will.

I was the one to look away first.

Jeremiah hung up the phone and asked Conrad, "Is Dan on his way to come get you?"

"Yeah. I'm just gonna hang out here and wait for him."

Jeremiah looked at me then. "What do you want to do?"

"I want to go with you," I said. I picked up my bag and Taylor's shoes.

He stood up and took my bag off my shoulder. "Then let's go." To Conrad, he said, "See you at home."

I wondered which home he meant, the summer house or their house-house. But I guessed it didn't really matter.

"Bye, Conrad," I said. I walked out the door with Taylor's shoes in my hand and I didn't bother to put them on either. I didn't look back. And right there, I felt it, the glow, the satisfaction of being the one who left first.

As we walked through the parking lot, Jeremiah said, "Maybe you should put your shoes on. You might cut your feet on something."

I shrugged. "They're Taylor's shoes," I said, as if that made sense. I added, "They're too small."

He asked, "Do you want to drive?"

I thought it over and then I said, "No, that's okay. You drive."

"But you love to drive my car," he said, coming around to the passenger side and opening my door first.

"I know. But today I just feel like riding shotgun."

"Do you want to get breakfast first?"

"No," I said. "I just want to go home."

Soon we were on the road. I opened my window all the way down. I stuck my head out and let my hair fly everywhere, just because. Steven once told me that bugs and things get caught up in girls' hair when they ride with it hanging out the window. But I didn't care. I liked the way it felt. It felt free.

Jeremiah looked over at me and said, "You remind me of our old dog, Boogie. He used to love riding around with his head out the window."

He was still using his polite voice. Distant.

I said, "You haven't said anything. About before." I glanced over at him. I could hear my heart thudding in my ears.

"What's left to say?"

"I don't know. A lot," I said.

"Belly—," he started. Then he stopped and let out a breath, shaking his head.

"What? What were you going to say?"

"Nothing," he said.

Then I reached across, and I took his hand and laced my fingers around his. It felt like the most right thing I'd done in a long time.

I worried he'd let go, but he didn't. We held hands like that the whole rest of the way home.

a couple of years later

When I used to picture forever, it was always with the same boy. In my dreams, my future was set. A sure thing.

This wasn't the way I pictured it. Me, in a white dress in the pouring rain, running for the car. Him, running ahead of me and opening the passenger door.

"Are you sure?" he asks me.

"No," I say, getting in.

The future is unclear. But it's still mine.

You never know what the summer will hold.

Turn the page for a sneak peek at the
final book in the *summer i turned pretty* trilogy

When it's finals week and you've been studying for five hours straight, you need three things to get you through the night. The biggest Slurpee you can find, half cherry, half Coke. Pajama pants, the kind that have been washed so many times, they are tissue-paper thin. And finally, dance breaks. Lots of dance breaks. When your eyes start to close and all you want is your bed, dance breaks will get you through.

It was four in the morning, and I was studying for the last final of my freshman year at Finch University. I was camped out in my dorm library with my new best friend, Anika Johnson, and my old best friend, Taylor Jewel. Summer vacation was so close, I could almost taste it. Just five more days. I'd been counting down since April.

"Quiz me," Taylor commanded, her voice scratchy.

I opened my notebook to a random page. "Define *anima* versus *animus*."

Taylor chewed on her lower lip. "Give me a hint."

"Umm . . . think Latin," I said.

"I didn't take Latin! Is there going to be Latin on this exam?"

"No, I was just trying to give you a hint. Because in Latin boys' names end in -*us* and girls' names end in -*a*, and *anima* is feminine archetype and *animus* is masculine archetype. Get it?"

She let out a big sigh. "No. I'm probably going to fail."

Looking up from her notebook, Anika said, "Maybe if you stopped texting and started studying, you wouldn't."

Taylor glared at her. "I'm helping my big sister plan our end-of-year breakfast, so I have to be on call tonight."

"On call?" Anika looked amused. "Like a doctor?"

"Yes, just like a doctor," Taylor snapped.

"So, will it be pancakes or waffles?"

"French toast, thank you very much."

The three of us were all taking the same freshman psych class, and Taylor's and my exam was tomorrow, Anika's was the day after. Anika was my closest friend at school besides Taylor. Seeing as how Taylor was competitive by nature, it was a friendship that she was more than a little jealous of, not that she'd ever in a million years admit it.

My friendship with Anika was different from my

friendship with Taylor. Anika was laid-back and easy to be with. She wasn't quick to judge. More than all that, though, she gave *me* the space to be different. She hadn't known me my whole life, so she had no expectations or preconceptions. There was freedom in that. And she wasn't like any of my friends back home. She was from New York, and her father was a jazz musician and her mother was a writer.

A couple of hours later, the sun was rising and casting the room in a bluish light, and Taylor's head was down, while Anika was staring off into space like a zombie.

I rolled up two paper balls in my lap and threw them at my two friends. "Dance break," I sang out as I pressed play on my computer. I did a little shimmy in my chair.

Anika glared at me. "Why are you so chipper?"

"Because," I said, clapping my hands together, "in just a few hours, it will all be over." My exam wasn't until one in the afternoon, so my plan was to go back to my room and sleep for a couple of hours, then wake up with time to spare and study some more.

I overslept, but I still managed to get another hour of studying in. I didn't have time to go to the dining hall for breakfast, so I just drank a Cherry Coke from the vending machine.

The test was as hard as we had expected, but I was pretty sure I would get at least a B. Taylor was pretty sure she hadn't failed, which was good. Both of us were too tired to celebrate after, so we just high-fived and went our separate ways.

I headed back to my dorm room, ready to pass out until at least dinnertime, and when I opened the door, there was Jeremiah, asleep in my bed. He looked like a little boy when he slept, even with the stubble. He was stretched out on top of my comforter, his feet hanging over the edge of the bed, my stuffed polar bear hugged to his chest.

I took off my shoes and crawled into my twin, extra-long bed next to him. He stirred, opened his eyes, and said, "Hi."

"Hi," I said.

"How'd it go?"

"Pretty good."

"Good." He let go of Junior Mint and hugged me to him. "I brought you the other half of my sub from lunch."

"You're sweet," I said, burrowing my head in his shoulder.

He kissed my hair. "I can't have my girl skipping meals left and right."

"It was just breakfast," I said. As an afterthought, I added, "And lunch."

"Do you want my sub now? It's in my book bag."

Now that I thought about it, I was hungry, but I was also sleepy. "Maybe a little later," I said, closing my eyes.

Then he fell back to sleep, and I fell asleep too. When I woke up, it was dark out, Junior Mint was on the floor, and Jeremiah's arms were around me. He was still asleep.

We had started dating right before I began senior year of high school. "Dating" didn't feel like the right word for it. We were just together. It all happened so easily and so quickly that it felt like it had always been that way. One minute we were friends, then we were kissing, and then the next thing I knew, I was applying to the same college as him. I told myself and everyone else (including him, including my mother especially) that it was a good school, that it was only a few hours from home and it made sense to apply there, that I was keeping my options open. All of those things were true. But truest of all was that I just wanted to be near him. I wanted him for all seasons, not just summer.

Now here we were, lying next to each other in my dorm-room bed. He was a sophomore, and I was a freshman finishing up my first year of college. It was crazy how far we had come. We'd known each other our whole lives, and in some ways, it felt like a big surprise, and in other ways it felt inevitable.

Jeremiah's fraternity was throwing an end-of-year party. In less than a week we would all go home for the summer, and we wouldn't be back at Finch until the end of August. I had always loved summertime best of all, but now that I was finally going home, somehow it felt a little bittersweet. I was used to meeting Jeremiah in the dining hall for breakfast every morning and doing my laundry with him at his frat house late at night. He was good at folding my T-shirts.

This summer, he would be interning at his dad's company again, and I was going to waitress at a family restaurant called Behrs, the same as I did last summer. Our plan was to meet at the summer house in Cousins as often as we could.

Last summer we hadn't made it out there once. We'd both been so busy with our jobs. I took every shift I could to save money for school. All the while, I'd felt a little hollow inside, my first summer away from Cousins.

There were a few lightning bugs out. It was just getting dark, and it wasn't too hot of a night. I was wearing heels, which was stupid, since on a last-minute impulse I'd walked instead of taking the bus. I just figured it was the last time for a long time I'd walk across campus on a nice night like this.

I'd invited Anika and our friend Shay to come with me, but Anika had a party with her dance team, and Shay was already done with finals and had flown home to Texas. Taylor's sorority was having a mixer, so she wasn't coming either. It was just me and my sore feet.

I had texted Jeremiah to tell him I was on my way and that I was walking, so it would take me a little while. I had to keep stopping to adjust my shoes because they were cutting into the backs of my feet. Heels were dumb, I decided.

Halfway there, I saw him sitting on my favorite bench. He stood up when he saw me. "Surprise!"

"You didn't have to meet me," I said, feeling very happy he had. I sat down on the bench.

"You look hot," he said.

Even now, after being boyfriend and girlfriend for a whole two years, I still blushed a little when he said things like that. "Thanks," I said. I was wearing a sundress that I had borrowed from Anika. It was white with little blue flowers and ruffly straps.

"That dress reminds me of *The Sound of Music*, but in a hot way."

"Thanks," I said again. *Did* the dress make me look like Fräulein Maria, I wondered? That didn't sound like a good thing. I smoothed down the straps a little.

A couple of guys I didn't recognize stopped and said hi to Jeremiah, but I stayed put on the bench so I could rest my feet.

When they were gone, he said, "Ready?"

I groaned. "My feet are killing me. Heels are dumb."

Jeremiah stooped down low and said, "Hop on, girl."

Giggling, I climbed on his back. I always giggled when he called me "girl." I couldn't help it. It was funny.

He hoisted me up, and I put my arms around his neck. "Is your dad coming on Monday?" Jeremiah asked as we crossed the main lawn.

"Yeah. You're gonna help, right?"

"Come on, now. I'm carrying you across campus. I have to help you move, too?"

I swatted him on the head and he ducked. "Okay, okay," he said.

Then I blew a raspberry on his neck, and he yelped like a little girl. I laughed the whole way there.

At Jeremiah's fraternity house, the doors were wide open and people were hanging out on the front lawn. Multi-colored Christmas lights were haphazardly strung all over the place—on the mailbox, the front porch, even along the edge of the walkway. They had three inflatable kiddie pools set up that people were lounging in like they were in hot tubs. Guys were running around with Super Soakers and spraying beer into each other's mouths. Some of the girls were in their bikinis.

I hopped off Jeremiah's back and took my shoes off in the grass.

"The pledges did a nice job with this," Jeremiah said, nodding appreciatively at the kiddie pools. "Did you bring your suit?"

I shook my head.

"Want me to see if one of the girls has an extra?" he offered.

Quickly, I said, "No thanks."

I knew Jeremiah's fraternity brothers from hanging out at the house, but I didn't know the girls very well. Most of them were from Zeta Phi, Jeremiah's fraternity's sister sorority. That meant they had mixers and parties together, that kind of thing. Jeremiah had wanted me to rush Zeta Phi, but I'd said no. I told him it was because I couldn't afford the fees and paying extra to live in a sorority house, but it was really more that I was hoping to be friends with all kinds of girls, not just the ones I'd meet in a sorority. I wanted a broader college experience, like my mother was always saying. According to Taylor, Zeta Phi was for party girls and sluts, as opposed to her sorority, which was allegedly classier and more exclusive. And way more focused on community service, she'd added as an afterthought.

Girls kept coming up and hugging Jeremiah. They said hi to me, and I said hi back, then I went upstairs to put my bag in Jeremiah's room. On my way back downstairs, I saw her.

Lacie Barone, wearing skinny jeans and a silky tank top and patent leather red heels that probably brought her up to five-four at most, talking to Jeremiah. Lacie was the social chair of Zeta Phi, and she was a junior—a year older than Jere, two years older than me. Her hair was dark brown, cut in a swishy bob, and she was petite. She was, by anybody's standards, hot. According to Taylor, she had a thing for Jeremiah. I told Taylor it didn't bother me one bit, and I meant it. Why should I care?

Of course girls would like Jeremiah. He was the kind of boy girls liked. But even a girl as pretty as Lacie didn't have anything on us. We were a couple years and years in the making. I knew him better than anyone, the same as he knew me, and I knew Jere would never look at another girl.

Jeremiah saw me then, and he waved at me to come over. I walked up to them and said, "Hey, Lacie."

"Hey," she said.

Pulling me toward him, Jeremiah said, "Lacie is gonna study abroad in Paris this fall." To Lacie, he said, "We want to go backpacking in Europe next summer."

Sipping her beer, she said, "That's cool. Which countries?"

"We're definitely going to France," Jeremiah said. "Belly speaks really fluent French."

"I actually don't," I told her, embarrassed. "I just took it in high school."

Lacie said, "Oh, I'm horrible too. I really just want to go and eat lots of cheese and chocolate."

She had a voice that was surprisingly husky for someone so small. I wondered if she smoked. She smiled at me, and I thought, Taylor was wrong about her, she was a nice girl.

When she left a few minutes later to get a drink, I said, "She's nice."

Jeremiah shrugged and said, "Yeah, she's cool. Want me to get you a drink?"

"Sure," I said.

He led me by the shoulders and planted me on the couch. "You sit right here. Don't move a muscle. I'll be right back."

I watched him make his way through the crowd, feeling proud I could call him mine. My boyfriend, my Jeremiah. The first boy I had ever fallen asleep next to. The first boy I ever told about the time I accidentally I walked in on my parents doing it when I was eight. The first boy to go out and buy me Midol because my cramps were so bad, the first boy to paint my toenails, to hold my hair back when I threw up that time I got really drunk in front of all his friends, the first boy to write me a love note on the whiteboard hanging outside my dorm room.

YOU ARE THE MILK TO MY SHAKE, forever and ever. Love, J.

He was the first boy I ever kissed. He was my best friend. More and more, I understood. This was the way it was supposed to be. He was the one. My one.

Read an excerpt from the first book of
Jenny Han's *New York Times* bestselling series
To All the Boys I've Loved Before

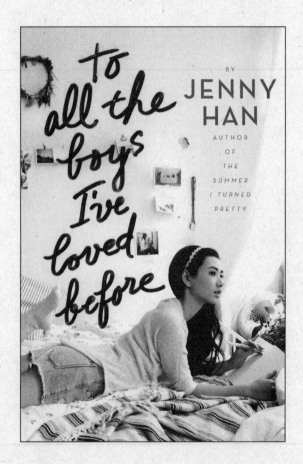

I like to save things. Not important things like whales or people or the environment. Silly things. Porcelain bells, the kind you get at souvenir shops. Cookie cutters you'll never use, because who needs a cookie in the shape of a foot? Ribbons for my hair. Love letters. Of all the things I save, I guess you could say my love letters are my most prized possession.

I keep my letters in a teal hatbox my mom bought me from a vintage store downtown. They aren't love letters that someone else wrote for me; I don't have any of those. These are ones I've written. There's one for every boy I've ever loved—five in all.

When I write, I hold nothing back. I write like he'll never read it. Because he never will. Every secret thought, every careful observation, everything I've saved up inside me, I put it all in the letter. When I'm done, I seal it, I address it, and then I put it in my teal hatbox.

They're not love letters in the strictest sense of the word. My letters are for when I don't want to be in love anymore. They're for good-bye. Because after I write my letter, I'm no longer consumed by my all-consuming love. I can eat my cereal and not wonder if he likes bananas over his Cheerios too; I can sing along to love songs and not be singing them to him. If love is like a possession, maybe my letters are like my exorcisms. My letters set me free. Or at least they're supposed to.

JOSH IS MARGOT'S BOYFRIEND, BUT I GUESS you could say my whole family is a little in love with him. It's hard to say who most of all. Before he was Margot's boyfriend, he was just Josh. He was always there. I say always, but I guess that's not true. He moved next door five years ago but it feels like always.

My dad loves Josh because he's a boy and my dad is surrounded by girls. I mean it: all day long he is surrounded by females. My dad is an ob-gyn, and he also happens to be the father of three daughters, so it's like girls, girls, girls all day. He also likes Josh because Josh likes comics and he'll go fishing with him. My dad tried to take us fishing once, and I cried when my shoes got mud on them, and Margot cried when her book got wet, and Kitty cried because Kitty was still practically a baby.

Kitty loves Josh because he'll play cards with her and not get bored. Or at least pretend to not get bored. They make deals with each other—if I win this next hand, you have to make me a toasted crunchy-peanut-butter-sandwich, no crusts. That's Kitty. Inevitably there won't be crunchy peanut butter and Josh will say too bad, pick something else. But then Kitty will wear him down and he'll run out and buy some, because that's Josh.

If I had to say why Margot loves him, I think maybe I would say it's because we all do.

We are in the living room, Kitty is pasting pictures of dogs to a giant piece of cardboard. There's paper and scraps all around her. Humming to herself, she says, "When Daddy asks me what I want for Christmas, I am just going to say, 'Pick any one of these breeds and we'll be good.'"

Margot and Josh are on the couch; I'm lying on the floor, watching TV. Josh popped a big bowl of popcorn, and I devote myself to it, handfuls and handfuls of it.

A commercial comes on for perfume: a girl is running around the streets of Paris in an orchid-colored halter dress that is thin as tissue paper. What I wouldn't give to be that girl in that tissue-paper dress running around Paris in springtime! I sit up so suddenly I choke on a kernel of popcorn. Between coughs I say, "Margot, let's meet in Paris for my spring break!" I'm already picturing myself twirling with a pistachio macaron in one hand and a raspberry one in the other.

Margot's eyes light up. "Do you think Daddy will let you?"

"Sure, it's culture. He'll have to let me." But it's true that I've never flown by myself before. And also I've never even left the country before. Would Margot meet me at the airport, or would I have to find my own way to the hostel?

Josh must see the sudden worry on my face because he says, "Don't worry. Your dad will definitely let you go if I'm with you."

I brighten. "Yeah! We can stay at hostels and just eat pastries and cheese for all our meals."

"We can go to Jim Morrison's grave!" Josh throws in.

"We can go to a *parfumerie* and get our personal scents done!" I cheer, and Josh snorts.

"Um, I'm pretty sure 'getting our scents done' at a *parfumerie* would cost the same as a week's stay at the hostel," he says. He nudges Margot. "Your sister suffers from delusions of grandeur."

"She is the fanciest of the three of us," Margot agrees.

"What about me?" Kitty whimpers.

"You?" I scoff. "You're the *least* fancy Song girl. I have to beg you to wash your feet at night, much less take a shower."

Kitty's face gets pinched and red. "I wasn't talking about that, you dodo bird. I was *talking* about Paris."

Airily, I wave her off. "You're too little to stay at a hostel."

She crawls over to Margot and climbs in her lap, even though she's nine and nine is too big to sit in people's laps. "Margot, you'll let me go, won't you?"

"Maybe it could be a family vacation," Margot says, kissing her cheek. "You and Lara Jean and Daddy could all come."

I frown. That's not at all the Paris trip I was imagining. Over Kitty's head Josh mouths to me, *We'll talk later*, and I give him a discreet thumbs-up.

It's later that night; Josh is long gone. Kitty and our dad are asleep. We are in the kitchen. Margot is at the table on her computer; I am sitting next to her, rolling cookie dough into balls and dropping them in cinnamon and sugar. Snickerdoodles to get back in Kitty's good graces. Earlier, when I went in to say good night, Kitty rolled over and wouldn't speak to me because she's still convinced I'm going to try to cut her out of the Paris trip. My plan is to put the snicker-doodles on a plate right next to her pillow so she wakes up to the smell of fresh-baked cookies.

Margot's being extra quiet, and then, out of nowhere, she looks up from her computer and says, "I broke up with Josh tonight. After dinner."

My cookie-dough ball falls out of my fingers and into the sugar bowl.

"I mean, it was time," she says. Her eyes aren't red-rimmed; she hasn't been crying, I don't think. Her voice is calm and even. Anyone looking at her would think she was fine. Because Margot is always fine, even when she's not.

"I don't see why you had to break up," I say. "Just 'cause you're going to college doesn't mean you have to break up."

"Lara Jean, I'm going to Scotland, not UVA. Saint Andrews is nearly four thousand miles away." She pushes up her glasses. "What would be the point?"

I can't even believe she would say that. "The point is, it's Josh. Josh who loves you more than any boy has ever loved a girl!"

Margot rolls her eyes at this. She thinks I'm being dra-matic, but I'm not. It's true—that's how much Josh loves Margot. He would never so much as look at another girl.

Suddenly she says, "Do you know what Mommy told me once?"

"What?" For a moment I forget all about Josh. Because

no matter what I am doing in life, if Margot and I are in the middle of an argument, if I am about to get hit by a car, I will always stop and listen to a story about Mommy. Any detail, any remembrance that Margot has, I want to have it too. I'm better off than Kitty, though. Kitty doesn't have one memory of Mommy that we haven't given her. We've told her so many stories so many times that they're hers now. "Remember that time . . . ," she'll say. And then she'll tell the story like she was there and not just a little baby.

"She told me to try not to go to college with a boyfriend. She said she didn't want me to be the girl crying on the phone with her boyfriend and saying no to things instead of yes."

Scotland is Margot's yes, I guess. Absently, I scoop up a mound of cookie dough and pop it in my mouth.

"You shouldn't eat raw cookie dough," Margot says.

I ignore her. "Josh would never hold you back from anything. He's not like that. Remember how when you decided to run for student-body president, he was your campaign manager? He's your biggest fan!"

At this, the corners of Margot's mouth turn down, and I get up and fling my arms around her neck. She leans her head back and smiles up at me. "I'm okay," she says, but she isn't, I know she isn't.

"It's not too late, you know. You can go over there right now and tell him you changed your mind."

Margot shakes her head. "It's done, Lara Jean." I release her and she closes her laptop. "When will the first batch be ready? I'm hungry."

I look at the magnetic egg timer on the fridge. "Four more minutes." I sit back down and say, "I don't care what you say, Margot. You guys aren't done. You love him too much."

She shakes her head. "Lara Jean," she begins, in her patient Margot voice, like I am a child and she is a wise old woman of forty-two.

I wave a spoonful of cookie dough under Margot's nose, and she hesitates and then opens her mouth. I feed it to her like a baby. "Wait and see, you and Josh will be back together in a day, maybe two." But even as I'm saying it, I know it's not true. Margot's not the kind of girl to break up and get back together on a whim; once she's decided something, that's it. There's no waffling, no regrets. It's like she said: when she's done, she's just done.

I wish (and this is a thought I've had many, many times, too many times to count) I was more like Margot. Because sometimes it feels like I'll never be done.

Later, after I've washed the dishes and plated the cookies and set them on Kitty's pillow, I go to my room. I don't turn the light on. I go to my window. Josh's light is still on.